ROUNDING THE MARK

ANDREA CAMILLERI

ROUNDING THE MARK

Translated by Stephen Sartarelli

PICADOR

First published 2006 by Penguin Books,
a member of Penguin Group (USA) Inc., New York

This edition first published in Great Britain 2007 by Picador
an imprint of Pan Macmillan Ltd
Pan Macmillan, 20 New Wharf Road, London N1 9RR
Basingstoke and Oxford
Associated companies throughout the world
www.panmacmillan.com

ISBN 978-0-330-44219-0 HB
ISBN 978-0-330-44725-6 TPB

Copyright © Sellerio Editore 2003
Translation copyright © Stephen Sartarelli 2006

Originally published in Italian as *Il giro di boa* by Sellerio Editore, Palermo.

The right of Andrea Camilleri to be identified as the
author of this work has been asserted by him in accordance
with the Copyright, Designs and Patents Act 1988.

1 3 5 7 9 8 6 4 2

A CIP catalogue record for this book is available from
the British Library.

Typeset by SetSystems Ltd, Saffron Walden, Essex
Printed and bound in Great Britain by
Mackays of Chatham plc, Chatham, Kent

Visit **www.panmacmillan.com** to read more about all our books
and to buy them. You will also find features, author interviews and
news of any author events, and you can sign up for e-newsletters
so that you're always first to hear about our new releases.

ROUNDING THE MARK

ONE

Stinking, treacherous night. Thrashing and turning, twisting and drifting off one minute, jolting awake and then lying back down — and it wasn't from having bolted down too much octopus *a strascinasali* or sardines *a beccafico* the evening before. No, he didn't even have that satisfaction. The evening before, his stomach had twisted up so tight that not even a blade of grass could have slipped through. It had all started when dark thoughts assailed him after he'd seen a story on the national evening news. When it rains it pours — *all'annigatu, petri di 'ncoddru* — or, 'rocks on a drowned man's back' as Sicilians call an unrelenting string of bad breaks that drag a poor man down. And since he'd been desperately flailing in storm-tossed seas for a few months now, feeling at times like he'd already drowned, that news had been like a big rock thrown right at him, at his head, in fact, knocking him out and finishing off what feeble strength he had left.

With an air of utter indifference, the anchor-woman

had announced, in reference to the police raid of the Diaz School during the G8 meetings in Genoa, that the public prosecutor's office of that city had concluded that the two Molotov cocktails found inside the school had been planted there by the policemen themselves, to justify the raid. This finding, continued the anchor-woman, came after the discovery that an officer who claimed to have been the victim of an attempted stabbing by an anti-globalist during the same raid had, in fact, been lying. The cut in his uniform turned out to have been made by the policeman himself, to show just how dangerous these kids were, and it was now emerging that the only thing those young people were doing at the Diaz School was sleeping peacefully. After hearing this news, Montalbano had sat there in his armchair for a good half-hour, unable to think, shaking with rage and shame, drenched in sweat. He hadn't even had the strength to get up and answer the telephone when it rang and rang. One needed only think a minute about this news — which the press and television were leaking out in dribs and drabs as the government watchfully looked on — and it became clear that his Genoese colleagues had committed an illegal action on the sly, a coldly calculated vendetta, fabricating evidence into the bargain, the sort of thing that brought to mind long-buried episodes of the Fascist police or the Scelba period.

Then he'd made up his mind and decided to go to bed. As he got up from the armchair, the telephone resumed its irritating refrain of rings. Without even realizing, he picked up the receiver. It was Livia.

'Salvo! My God, I've tried calling you so many times! I was starting to get worried! Couldn't you hear the phone?'

'I could, but I didn't feel like answering. I didn't know it was you.'

'What were you doing?'

'Nothing. Thinking about what I'd just seen on television.'

'You mean what happened in Genoa?'

'Yeah.'

'Oh. I saw the news, too.' She paused, then: 'I wish I was there with you. Do you want me to catch a plane tomorrow and come down? That way we could talk in peace. You'll see—'

'Livia, there's not much left to say at this point. We've talked it over many times these last few months. This time I'm serious. I've made my decision.'

'What decision?'

'I'm resigning. Tomorrow I'm going to go and talk to Commissioner Bonetti-Alderighi and give him my resignation. I'm sure he'll be delighted.'

Livia did not immediately react, and Montalbano thought perhaps they'd been cut off.

'Hello, Livia? Are you there?'

'I'm here. Salvo, in my opinion you're making a big mistake to leave this way.'

'What way?'

'Out of anger and disappointment. You want to leave the police force because you feel betrayed, as if the person you trusted most—'

'Livia, I don't *feel* betrayed, I *have been* betrayed. We're not talking about feelings here. I've always done my job honourably. With integrity. If I gave a crook my word, I kept it. And that's why I'm respected. That's been my strength, can you understand that? But now I'm fed up, I'm sick of it all.'

'Please don't yell,' said Livia, her voice quavering.

Montalbano didn't hear her. There was a strange noise inside him, as if his blood had reached boiling point. He continued:

'I never once fabricated evidence, not even against the worst criminals! Never! If I had, I would have been stooping to their level. And then you really could have said that this is a filthy job! Do you realize what happened, Livia? The people attacking that school and planting false evidence weren't a bunch of stupid, violent beat policemen; they were commissioners and vice-commissioners, inspectors and captains and other paragons of virtue!'

Only then did he realize that the noise he was hearing in the receiver was Livia sobbing. He took a deep breath.

'Livia?'

'Yes?'

'I love you. Goodnight.'

He hung up. Then he went to bed. And the treacherous night began.

*

The truth of the matter was that Montalbano's malaise had set in a while back, when the television had first shown the Prime Minister strolling up and down the narrow streets of Genoa, tidying the flower boxes and ordering the inhabitants to remove the underwear hung out to dry on balconies and windowsills while his Interior Minister was adopting security measures more suited for an imminent civil war than for a meeting of heads of state: setting up wire fences to block access to certain streets, soldering shut the manholes, sealing the country's borders, closing certain railway stations, establishing boat patrols at sea, and even installing a battery of missiles. This was such an excessive display of defence, thought the inspector, that it became a kind of provocation. Then what happened, happened: one of the demonstrators got killed, of course, but perhaps the worst of it was that certain police units had thought it best to fire tear gas at the most peaceable demonstrators, leaving the most violent ones, the so-called 'black bloc', free to do as they pleased. Then came the ugly episode at the Diaz School, which resembled not so much a police operation as a wicked and violent abuse of power with the sole purpose of venting a repressed lust for revenge.

*

Three days after the G8, as polemics raged all over Italy, Montalbano had arrived late to work. No sooner had he pulled up in his car and got out, than he'd noticed two painters whitewashing one of the walls outside the station.

'Ahh, Chief, Chief!' cried Catarella, seeing him come in. 'They wrote us some nasty things last night!'

Montalbano didn't immediately understand.

'Who wrote to us?'

'I don't poissonally know them that writ 'em.'

What the hell was Catarella talking about?

'Was it anonymous?'

'No, Chief, it wasn't on nominus, it was onna wall outside. An' 'at was why Fazio, foist ting this morning, called for the painers to come cover it up.'

At last the inspector understood why the two painters were there.

'What'd they write on the wall?'

Catarella turned beetroot red and attempted an evasion.

'They wrote some bad words with black spray paint.'

'Yeah, like what?'

'Sleazeball cops,' replied Catarella, keeping his eyes lowered.

'Is that all?'

'No, sir. They also wrote "murderers". Sleazeballs and murderers.'

'Why you taking it so hard, Cat?'

Catarella looked like he was about to burst into tears.

''Cause nobody in here's no sleazeball or murderer,

startin' wit' you, sir, and endin' wit' me, the smallest wheel on the cart.'

By way of consolation, Montalbano patted Catarella's shoulder and headed towards his office. Catarella called him back.

'Oh, Chief! I almost forgot. They also wrote "goddamn cuckolds".'

Imagine ever finding any obscene graffiti in Sicily without the word 'cuckold' in it! The word was a guarantee of authenticity, a classic expression of so-called Sicilitude. The inspector had just sat down when Mimì Augello came in. He was cool as a cucumber, his face relaxed and serene.

'Any news?' he asked.

'Did you hear what they wrote on the wall last night?'

'Yeah, Fazio told me.'

'Doesn't that seem like news to you?'

Mimì gave him a befuddled look.

'Are you joking or serious?'

'I'm serious.'

'Well, then, swear to me on a stack of Bibles. Do you think Livia cheats on you?'

This time it was Montalbano who gave Mimì a puzzled look.

'What the fuck are you talking about?'

'So you're not a cuckold. And I don't think Beba cheats on me, either. OK, on to the next word: sleazeball. True, two or three women have called me a sleaze, I won't deny it. But I bet nobody's ever called you one, so that word doesn't refer to you. Murderer, forget it. So what's the problem?'

'Well, aren't you the razor wit, with your Sunday crossword-puzzle logic!'

'Wait a second, Salvo. Is this somehow the first time we've been called bastards, sons of bitches, and murderers?'

'The difference is that this time, it's true.'

'Ah, so that's how you see it?'

'Yes, it is. Explain to me why we acted that way in Genoa, after years and years without any incidents of that sort.'

Mimì looked at him, eyelids drooping so low that they nearly covered his eyes, and said nothing.

'Oh, no you don't!' said the inspector. 'Answer me verbally, not with that little "cop stare" of yours.'

'All right. But first I want to make something clear. I'm in no mood to pick any bones with you. OK?'

'OK.'

'I know what's bugging you. The fact that all this happened under a government that you don't trust and openly oppose. You think the political leaders are up to their necks in this affair.'

'Excuse me, Mimì, but have you read the newspapers? Have you watched the TV news? They have all said, more or less clearly, that at the time, there were people in the command rooms in Genoa that had no business being there: ministers, members of Parliament, all from the same party.

conversations with Livia, the wound the inspector carried inside him was beginning at last to heal when he got wind of another brilliant police action, this time in Naples. A handful of cops had been arrested for forcibly removing some allegedly violent political activists from a hospital into which they'd been admitted. After bringing them to a barracks, the police treated them to a flurry of kicks and punches and a torrent of obscenities and insults. But what most upset Montalbano was the reaction of other police-men to the news of their colleagues' arrest. Some chained themselves to the gate of the Central Police building in an act of solidarity; others organized demonstrations in the streets; the unions made some noise; and a deputy com-missioner who in Genoa had kicked a demonstrator already on the ground was greeted as a hero when he came to Naples. The same politicians who'd been in Genoa for the G8 were behind this curious (though not so curious for Montalbano) semi-revolt on the part of the forces of order against the judges who had issued the arrest warrants. And Montalbano couldn't take it any more. This last, bitter morsel he just couldn't swallow. One morning, as soon as he got to work, he called Dr Lattes, chief of the Montelusa police commissioner's cabinet. Half an hour later, Lattes informed him, through Catarella, that the commissioner could see him at twelve noon on the dot. The men at the station, who had learned to gauge their boss's mood from the way he walked into the office each morning, realized at once that this was not a good day. And so, from the vantage point of Montalbano's desk, the station seemed deserted that morning. No voices, no sounds whatsoever. Catarella was standing guard at the entrance door, and as soon as anyone came in, he opened his eyes wide, put his forefinger over his nose, and enjoined the intruder to silence.

'Ssssshhhh!'

All who entered the station acted like they were attending a wake.

Around ten o'clock, Mimì Augello, after knocking discreetly and being told to come in, entered the inspector's office with a grim expression on his face. As soon as he saw him, Montalbano got worried.

'How's Beba doing?'

'Fine. Can I sit down?'

'Of course.'

'Can I smoke?'

'Of course, but don't let the minister see you.'

Augello fired up a cigarette, inhaled, and held the smoke in his lungs a long time.

'You can exhale now,' said Montalbano. 'You have my permission.'

Mimì looked at him, confused.

'Yes,' the inspector continued, 'this morning you seem Chinese to me. You ask my permission for every little thing. What's wrong? Is it so hard to tell me what you want to tell me?'

'Yes,' Augello admitted. He put out his cigarette, got more comfortable in his chair, and began, 'Salvo, you know I've always thought of you as my father—'

'Where'd you get that idea?'

'Where'd I get what idea?'

'That I'm your father. If it was your mother who told you, she's a liar. I'm fifteen years older than you, and though I may have been precocious, at age fifteen I wasn't—'

'Salvo, I didn't say you were my father, I said I thought of you as a father.'

'And you got off on the wrong foot. Drop the Father, Son, and Holy Ghost shit. Just say what you have to say and get the hell out of my hair, 'cause today's not a good day.'

'Why did you ask to see the commissioner?'

'Who told you that?'

'Catarella.'

'I'll deal with him later.'

'No, you won't. If anything, you'll deal with me right now. I was the one who told Catarella to tell me if you contacted Bonetti-Alderighi, which I expected you would do sooner or later.'

'But what's so unusual about me, an inspector, wanting to talk to my superior?'

'Salvo, you know you can't stand Bonetti-Alderighi. You hate his guts. If he was a priest at your deathbed wanting to give you last rites, you'd get up out of bed and kick him out of your room. I'm gonna talk to you straight, OK?'

'Talk however the fuck you like.'

'You want to leave.'

'A little holiday would do me some good.'

'You're unbearable, Salvo. You want to resign.'

'Don't I have the right?' Montalbano burst out, sitting up at the edge of his chair, ready to leap to his feet.

Augello wasn't intimidated.

'You have every right. But first let me finish telling you what I have to say. Remember when you said you had a suspicion?'

'A suspicion of what?'

'That the events in Genoa had been deliberately provoked by a political faction that in one way or another had promised to protect the police. Remember?'

'Yes.'

'Well, I just want to point out to you that what happened in Naples happened when there was a Centre-Left government in power, before the G8 meetings. We just didn't find out about it till later. What do you make of that?'

'That makes it even worse. Do you think I haven't thought about these things, Mimì? It means the whole problem is a lot more serious than we realize.'

'How's that?'

'It means the rot is inside us.'

'Did you just find that out today? With all the books

you've read? If you want to leave, go ahead and leave. But not right now. Leave because you're tired, because you've reached the age limit, because your haemorrhoids hurt, because your brain can't function any more, but don't quit now.'

'And why not?'

'Because it would be an insult.'

'An insult to whom?'

'To me, for one — and I may be a womanizer, but I'm a decent man. To Catarella, who's an angel. To Fazio, who's a classy guy. To everybody who works for the Vigàta Police. To Commissioner Bonetti-Alderighi, who's a pain in the arse and a formalist, but deep down is a good person. To all your colleagues who admire you and are your friends. To the great majority of people who work for the police and have nothing to do with the handful of rogues at the top and the bottom of the totem pole. You're slamming the door in all of our faces. Think about it. See you later.'

He got up, opened the door, and went out. At eleven thirty Montalbano had Catarella ring up the commissioner's office. He told Dr Lattes he wouldn't be coming; the thing he had to tell him was of little importance, no importance at all.

After phoning, he felt the need for some sea air. Passing by the switchboard, he said to Catarella:

'Now run off and report to Inspector Augello.'

Catarella looked at him like a beaten dog.

'Why do you wanna insult me, Chief?'

Insult him. Everyone was feeling insulted by him, but he wasn't allowed to feel insulted by anyone.

*

All of a sudden he couldn't stand to lie in bed another minute, hashing and rehashing the words he'd exchanged with Mimì over the last few days. Hadn't he communicated his decision to Livia? What was done was done. He turned towards the window. A faint light filtered in. The clock said a few minutes before six. He got up and opened the shutters. To the east, the glow of the imminent sunrise sketched arabesques of wispy, rainless clouds. The sea was a little stirred up by the morning breeze. He let the air fill his lungs, feeling a bit of his treacherous night being carried off with each exhalation. He went in the kitchen, filled the coffee pot and, while waiting for it to boil, opened the doors to the veranda.

The beach — at least as far as the eye could see through the haze — looked deserted by man and beast. He drank two cups of coffee, one right after the other, put on his swimming trunks, and went down to the beach. The sand was wet and compacted; maybe it had rained during the night. At the water's edge, he stuck his foot out. The water felt a lot less icy than he had feared. He advanced warily, cold shudders running up his spine. *Why, at over fifty years of age, do I keep trying to do these stunts?* he asked himself. *I'll probably end up with one of those colds that numbs my head and has me sneezing for a week.*

He began swimming in slow, broad strokes. The sea smelt harsh, stinging his nostrils like champagne, and he nearly got drunk on it. Montalbano kept swimming and swimming, his head finally free of all thought, happy to have turned into a kind of mechanical doll. He was jolted back to human reality when a cramp suddenly bit into his left calf. Cursing the saints, he flipped onto his back and did the dead man's float. The pain was so sharp that it made him grit his teeth. Sooner or later it would pass. These damned cramps had become more frequent in the last two or three years. Signs of old age lurking round the corner? The current carried him lazily along. The pain was starting to abate, and this allowed him to take two arm-strokes backwards. At the end of the second stroke, his hand struck something.

In a fraction of a second, Montalbano realized he'd struck a human foot. Somebody else was floating right beside him, and he hadn't noticed.

'Excuse me,' he said hastily, flipping back onto his belly and looking over at the other.

The person beside him didn't answer, however, because he wasn't doing the dead man's float. He was actually dead. And, to judge from the way he looked, he'd been so for quite a while.

TWO

Flummoxed, Montalbano started swimming around the body, trying not to make waves with his arms. There was sufficient light now, and the cramp had passed. The corpse certainly wasn't fresh. It must have been in the water for quite some time, since there wasn't much flesh left attached to the bone. The head looked practically like a skull. A skull with seaweed for hair. The right leg was coming detached from the rest of the body. The fish and the sea had made a shambles of the poor wretch, probably a castaway or non-European who'd been driven by hunger or despair to try his luck as an illegal immigrant and been chucked overboard by some slave trader a little slimier and nastier than the rest. Yes, that corpse must have hailed from far away. Was it possible that the whole time it had been floating out there not a single trawler, or any boat at all, had noticed it? Unlikely. No doubt somebody had seen it but had promptly fallen in line with the new morality, whereby if you run over someone in your car, for example, you're supposed to speed away and lend no aid. Fat chance a trawler would stop for something so useless as a corpse. Anyway, hadn't there been some fishermen who, upon finding human remains in their nets, had promptly dumped them back in the sea to avoid bureaucratic hassles? 'Pity is dead', as some song or poem, or whatever the hell it was, once said, a long time ago. And, little by little, compassion, brotherhood, solidarity, and respect for the elderly, the sick, and little children were also dying out, along with the rules of—

Cut the moralistic crap, Montalbano said to himself, *and try instead to find a way out of this pickle.*

Rousing himself from his thoughts, he looked towards land. Jesus, it was far! How had he ended up so far out? And how the hell was he ever going to tow that corpse ashore? The corpse, meanwhile, had drifted a few yards away, dragged by the current. Was it challenging him to a swimming race? At that moment the solution to the problem came to him. He took off his bathing suit, which, in addition to the elastic waistband, had a long rope around the waist that was purely ornamental and served no purpose. In two strokes he was beside the corpse; after reflecting for a moment, he slipped the bathing suit over the body's left arm, wrapped it tightly around the wrist, then bound it with one end of the rope. With the other end he tied two firm knots around his own left ankle. If the corpse's arm didn't fall off as he was towing it − a very distinct possibility − the whole ordeal might, he was sure, come to a peaceful, happy ending, albeit at the cost of tremendous physical effort.

He began to swim. And for a long stretch he swam rather slowly, necessarily using only his arms, stopping from time to time to catch his breath, or to see if the corpse was still attached to him. Slightly more than half-way to shore, he had to stop for a little longer than usual; he was huffing and puffing like a bellows. When he turned onto his back to do the dead man's float, the dead man — the real one, that is — flipped face-down from the movement conveyed to him through the rope.

'Please be patient,' Montalbano excused himself.

When his panting had subsided a little, he set off again. After a spell that seemed endless, he realized he had reached a point where he could touch bottom. Slipping the rope off his foot but hanging on to it with one hand, he stood up. The water came up to his nose. Hopping on tiptoe, he advanced a few more yards until he could finally rest his feet flat on the sand. At this point, feeling safe at last, he tried to take a step forward.

Try as he might, he couldn't move. He tried again. Nothing. Oh God, he'd become paralysed! He was like a post planted in the middle of the water, a post with a corpse moored to it. On the beach there wasn't a soul to whom he might cry for help. Was it maybe all a dream, a nightmare?

Now I'm going to wake up, he told himself.

But he did not wake up. In despair, he threw his head back and let out a yell so loud that it deafened him. The yell produced two immediate results: the first was that a pair of seagulls hovering over his head and enjoying the farce took fright and flew away; the second was that his muscles and nerves – in short, his whole bodily mechanism – started moving again, though with extreme difficulty. Another thirty steps separated him from the shore, but they were like the climb up Mount Calvary. When he reached the beach, he dropped to the ground, on his arse, and stayed that way, still holding the rope in his hand. He looked like a fisherman unable to drag ashore an oversized fish he'd just caught. He consoled himself with the thought that the worst was over.

'Hands in the air!' a voice cried out behind him.

Befuddled, Montalbano turned his head to look. The person who had spoken, and who was taking aim at him with a revolver that must have dated from the Italo-Turkish War (1911–12), was a reed-thin, nervous man over seventy years old with wild eyes and sparse hair sticking straight up like iron wire. Next to him was a woman, also past seventy, wearing a straw hat and holding an iron rod that she kept shaking, either as a threat or because she suffered from advanced Parkinson's disease.

'Just a minute,' said Montalbano. 'I'm—'

'You're a murderer!' shouted the woman in a voice so shrill that the seagulls, who in the meantime had gathered to enjoy Act II of the farce, darted away, shrieking.

'But, signora, I'm—'

'It's no use denying it, you murderer, I've been watching you through my binoculars for the past two hours!' she shouted, even louder than before.

Montalbano felt totally at sea. Without thinking of what he was doing, he dropped the rope, turned around, and stood up.

'Oh my God! He's naked!' the old lady screamed, taking two steps back.

'You swine! You're a dead man!' the old man screamed, taking two steps back.

And he fired. The deafening shot passed some twenty yards away from the inspector, who was more frightened by the blast than anything else. Knocked another two steps back by the pistol's kick, the old man stubbornly took aim again.

'What are you doing? Are you crazy? I'm—'

'Shut up and don't move!' the old man ordered him. 'We've called the police. They'll be here any minute now.'

Montalbano didn't budge. Out of the corner of his eye he saw the corpse slowly heading back out to sea. When the Lord was good and ready, two speeding cars pulled up with a screech. Seeing Fazio and Gallo, both in civilian dress, get out of the first one, Montalbano took heart. But not for long, because out of the second car stepped a photographer who immediately began shooting, rapid-fire. Recognizing the inspector at once, Fazio shouted to the old man:

'Police! Don't shoot!'

'How do I know you're not his accomplices?' was the man's reply.

And he pointed his pistol at Fazio. But in so doing, he

took his eye off Montalbano, who, feeling fed up by this point, sprang forward, grabbed the old man's wrist, and disarmed him. He was not, however, able to dodge the fierce blow dealt him to the head by the old lady with her iron rod. All at once his vision fogged, his knees buckled, and he passed out.

*

After losing consciousness, he must have drifted into sleep, since when he awoke in his bed and looked at the clock, it was eleven thirty. The first thing he did was sneeze, one sneeze after another after still another. He'd caught a cold, and his head hurt like hell. He heard Adelina, his housekeeper, call to him from the kitchen.

'You awake, signore?'

'Yes, but my head hurts. Want to bet the old lady broke it?'

'Even bombs couldna break dat head of yours, signore.'

The telephone rang. He tried to get up, but a sort of vertigo knocked him back down into bed. How could that old bag have had such strength in her arms? Adelina, meanwhile, answered the phone. He heard her saying:

'He jes' woke uppa now. OK, I tell him.'

She appeared with a steaming cup of coffee in her hand.

'Dat was Signor Fazziu. He says he comma to see you here in haffa nour atta most.'

'Adelì, what time did you get here?'

'At nine, as usual, signore. They ha' put you inna bed, an' Signor Gallu he stay behind to help. So I says, now I'm here, I can look afta you, an' so he left.'

She went out of the room and came back with a glass in one hand and a pill in the other.

'I brung you some aspirin.'

Obediently, Montalbano took it. Sitting up in bed, he felt a few chills run through his body. Adelina noticed and, muttering to herself, opened the armoire, grabbed a tartan blanket, and spread it over the bedspread.

'At your age, signore, you got no business doin' them kinda things.'

At that moment, Montalbano loathed her. He pulled the blanket up over his head and closed his eyes.

*

He heard the telephone ringing repeatedly. Why didn't Adelina answer it? He staggered to his feet and went into the living room.

'H'lo?' he said in a congested voice.

'Inspector? Fazio here. I can't come, I'm sorry to say. There's been a snag.'

'Anything serious?'

'No, little shit. I'll drop by in the afternoon. You take care of that cold in the meantime.'

He hung up and went in the kitchen. Adelina was gone. She'd left a note on the table.

You was sleeping and I din't wanna wake you up. Annyway signor Fazziu's gonna come soon. I make some food and put it in the fridge. Adelina.

He didn't feel like opening the refrigerator. He had no appetite. Realizing he was walking around naked as Adam, he put on a shirt, a pair of underpants, and some trousers, and sat down in his usual armchair in front of the TV. It was a quarter to one, time for the lunchtime news on TeleVigàta, a pro-government station whether the government was of the extreme Left or extreme Right. The first thing he saw was himself, stark naked, wild-eyed, mouth agape, hands cupped over his pudenda, looking like a chaste Susannah getting on in years, and a whole lot hairier. A caption under the image said:

'Inspector Montalbano (in the photo) saving a dead man.'

Montalbano remembered the photographer who had arrived behind Fazio and Gallo, and sent him, in his mind, best wishes for a long and prosperous life. Then the purse-lipped, chicken-arse face of Pippo Ragonese, the inspector's sworn enemy, appeared on the screen.

'Shortly after sunrise this morning . . .'

For those who might not understand, a generic shot of a sunrise appeared.

'. . . our hero, Inspector Salvo Montalbano, went out for a nice long swim . . .'

A stretch of sea appeared, with some guy swimming far in the distance, tiny and unrecognizable.

'You're probably thinking that not only is it no longer the season for swimming, but it's not really the most appropriate time of day for it, either. But what are you going to do? That's our hero for you. Maybe he felt the need to take a dip to dispel the strange ideas that are often swirling about in his brain. Swimming far offshore, he ran into the corpse of an unknown man. Instead of calling the authorities . . .'

'. . . with the mobile phone installed in my dick,' Montalbano chimed in, enraged.

'. . . our inspector decided to tow the corpse to shore without anyone's help, tying it to his leg with the bathing suit he was wearing. "I can do it all myself," that's his motto. These manoeuvres did not escape the attention of Signora Pina Bausan, who had been looking out to sea with a pair of binoculars.'

On-screen appeared the face of Signora Bausan, the lady who'd cracked his skull with an iron bar.

'Where are you from, signora?'

'My husband Angelo and I are both from Treviso.'

'Have you been in Sicily long?'

'We got here four days ago.'

'On holiday?'

'This is no holiday, believe me. I suffer from asthma, and my doctor told me that some sea air would do me good. My daughter Zina is married to a Sicilian who works in Treviso . . .' Here Signora Bausan interrupted her speech with a long, pained sigh, as if to lament the fate that had given her a Sicilian for a son-in-law. 'And she told me to come and stay here, at her husband's house, which they use only one month out of the year, in the summer. So we came.'

The pained sigh was even longer this time. Life is so hard and dangerous on that savage island!

'Tell me, signora, why were you looking out to sea at that hour?'

'I get up early, and I have to do something, don't I?'

'And you, Signor Bausan, do you always carry that weapon with you?'

'No, I don't own any weapons. I borrowed that pistol from a cousin of mine. Since we were coming to Sicily, you understand . . .'

'So you think one should come to Sicily armed?'

'If there's no rule of law down here, it seems logical, don't you think?'

Ragonese's purse-lipped face reappeared on the screen.

'And this gave rise to a huge misunderstanding. Believing—'

Montalbano turned it off. He felt enraged at Bausan, not for having shot at him, but for what he had said. He picked up the phone.

'H'lo, Cadarella?'

'Listen, you motherfucking sonofabitch—'

'Hey, Cad, dode you regogdize me? Id's Modtadbado.'

'Ah, izzat you, Chief? You gotta cold?'

'No, Cad, I just like talking this way. Lebbe talk to Fadzio.'

'Straight away, Chief.'

Fazio's voice came on the line: 'What is it, Chief?'

'Fazio, what ever happedd to the ode mad's pistol?'

'You mean Bausan's? I gave it back to him.'

'Has he god a licence for it?'

There was an embarrassed silence.

'I don't know, Chief. In all that confusion, it slipped my mind.'

'All righd. I mead, it's dot all righd. I wad you to go fide this mad, righd this middit, and see if his papers are id order. If they're dot, you're to edforce the law. We cad't let sub sedile ode geezer go aroud shooding eddythig that booves.'

'Got it, Chief.'

Done. That would show Signor Bausan and his charming wife that, even in Sicily, there were a few laws. Just a few, but laws all the same. He was about to get back in bed when the phone rang.

'H'lo?'

'Salvo, darling, what's wrong with your voice? Were you sleeping or are you sick?'

'The ladder.'

'I tried your office, but they said you were at home. Tell me what happened.'

'Whad do you wad me to say? It was like sub cobbedy routeed. I was daked and the guy shod ad me. Add zo I gaughd a gode.'

'You you you you—'

'Whad's "youyouyouyou" mead?'

'You ... took off your clothes in front of the commissioner and he shot you?'

Montalbano balked.

'And why would I wad to take my clodes off id frod of the cobbissioder?'

'Because last night you said that this morning, come hell or high water, you were going to hand in your resignation!'

With his free hand, Montalbano slapped his forehead hard. His resignation! He'd forgotten all about it!

'Whad happedd, Livia, is, dis mordig, I was doig the dead mad's float whed a dead mad—'

'Goodbye, Salvo,' Livia said testily. 'I have to go to work. Call me when you can talk again.'

The only thing to do was to take another aspirin, get under the covers, and sweat like a pig.

Before entering the country of sleep, he began to review, quite involuntarily, his whole encounter with the corpse.

When he got to the point where he raised the body's arm to slip his bathing suit over it, then wrapped the garment tightly around the wrist, the film in his brain stopped and then backed up, as on an editing table. Arm raised, bathing suit slipped over arm, bathing suit wrapped tight ... Stop. Arm raised, bathing suit slipped over arm ... Then sleep won.

*

At six that evening he was on his feet. He'd slept like a baby and felt nearly recovered from his cold. He had to be patient, however, and stay home for the rest of the day.

He still felt tired, and he knew why. It was the combined effect of the treacherous night, the swim, the exertion of towing the corpse to land, the iron rod to the head, and, above all, the drop in tension from not having gone to see the commissioner. He locked himself in the bathroom, took an extremely long shower, shaved with great care, and got dressed as if to go to the office. But, calm and determined, he phoned the commissioner's office instead.

'Hello? Inspector Montalbano here. I want to speak to the commissioner. It's urgent.'

He had to wait a few seconds.

'Montalbano? This is Lattes. How are you? How's the family?'

Good God, what a pain in the arse! This Dr Lattes, informally known as 'Caffè-Lattes', was an avid reader of such publications as *L'Avvenire* and *Famiglia Cristiana*. He was convinced that any respectable man had to have a wife and children. And since, in his own way, he admired Montalbano, he simply couldn't get it into his head that the inspector wasn't married.

'They're all fine, thanking the Lord,' said Montalbano.

By now he'd learned that invoking the Lord was the best way to achieve maximum cooperation on Lattes's part.

'What can I do for you?'

'I'd like to confer with the commissioner.'

Confer! Montalbano felt a twinge of self-loathing. But when dealing with bureaucrats it was best to talk like them.

'The commissioner's not in. He was summoned to Rome by (*pause*) His Excellency the Minister of Justice.'

The pause – Montalbano could see it clearly in his mind's eye – had been prompted by Dr Lattes's respectful need to stand to attention when invoking His Excellency the Minister.

'Oh,' said Montalbano, feeling his body go limp. 'Do you know how long he'll be away?'

'Another two or three days, I think. Can I be of any help?'

'Thank you, Doctor, it's all right. I can wait till he returns.'

E passeranno i giorni ... he sang to himself angrily, slamming down the receiver. The minute he decided to hand in – or rather, to use the proper expression, to *tender* – his resignation, something arose to thwart his intention.

He realized that, despite his fatigue, which was aggravated by the phone call, he felt hungry as a wolf. It was ten past six, not yet dinner time. But who ever said you have to eat at an appointed time of day? He went into the kitchen and opened the refrigerator. Adelina had prepared a dish fit for a convalescent: boiled cod. On the other hand, they were huge, extremely fresh, and six in number. He didn't bother to reheat them; he liked them cold, dressed with olive oil, a few drops of lemon, and salt. Adelina had bought the bread that morning: a round *scanata* loaf covered with *giuggiulena*, those delicious sesame seeds you are supposed to eat one by one as they fall onto the tablecloth, picking them up with your forefinger moistened by saliva. He set the table on the veranda and had a feast, savouring each bite as though it was his last.

When he cleared the table, it was a little past eight. So now what was he going to do to kill time until bedtime? The question was answered at once when Fazio knocked at the door.

'Good evening, Chief. I'm here to report. How are you feeling?'

'A lot better, thanks. Have a seat. What did you do with Bausan?'

Fazio got comfortable in his chair, pulled a small piece of paper out of his pocket, and began to read.

'Angelo Bausan, son of the late Angelo Bausan senior and Angela Crestin, born at—'

'Nothing but angels up there,' the inspector interrupted. 'But now you have to decide. Either you put that piece of paper back in your pocket, or I'm going to start kicking you.'

Fazio suppressed his 'records office complex', as the inspector called it, put the piece of paper back in his pocket with dignity, and said:

'After you called, Chief, I immediately went to the house where Angelo Bausan is staying. It's a few hundred yards from here and belongs to his son-in-law, Maurizio Rotondò. Bausan's got no gun licence. But you have no idea what I had to go through to get him to turn in his pistol. His wife even bashed me on the head with a broom. And a broom, in Signora Bausan's hands, becomes an improvised weapon. That old lady is so strong ... You know a little about that yourself.'

'Why didn't he want to give you the gun?'

'Because he said he had to give it back to the friend who lent it to him. The friend's name is Roberto Pausin. I sent his vital statistics on to Treviso Police and put the old man in jail. He's the judge's baby now.'

'Any news on the corpse?'

'The one you found?'

'What other ones are there?'

'Look, Chief, while you were here recovering, two more bodies were found in or around Vigàta.'

'I'm interested in the one I found.'

'No news, Chief. He must have been an illegal alien who drowned before reaching land. In any case, Dr Pasquano's probably done the post-mortem by now.'

As if on cue, the telephone rang.

'You answer,' said Montalbano.

Fazio reached out and picked up the receiver.

'Inspector Montalbano's residence. Who am I? I'm Sergeant Fazio. Oh, it's you? Sorry, I didn't recognize your voice. I'll put him on right away.' He handed the inspector the receiver. 'It's Pasquano.'

Pasquano? When had Dr Pasquano ever called him at home before? It must be something big.

THREE

'Hello? Montalbano here. What is it, Doctor?'

'Could you explain something for me?'

'I'm at your service.'

'How is it that every other time you've kindly sent a corpse my way, you busted my balls demanding immediately to know the results of the post-mortem, and this time you don't give a flying fuck?'

'Well, what happened is—'

'I'll tell you what happened. You decided that the dead body you hauled ashore belonged to some poor third-world bastard whose boat had capsized, one of the five hundred-plus corpses that are lately so crowding the Sicilian Channel that you can practically walk to Tunisia across the water. And you just washed your hands of it. Since, one more, one less, what's the difference?'

'Doctor, if you want to vent your frustrations on me for something that didn't go right, be my guest. But you know perfectly well that's not how I feel about these things. Furthermore, this morning—'

'Ah, yes, this morning you were busy displaying your masculine attributes for the "Mr Police Universe" competition. I saw you on TeleVigàta. I'm told you got very high — what're they called? — very high audience ratings. My sincerest compliments.'

Pasquano was like that. Crass, obnoxious, aggressive, off-putting. The inspector knew, however, that it was an instinctive, exasperated form of self-defence against everyone and everything. Montalbano counter-attacked, adopting the requisite tone of voice.

'Doctor, could you tell me why you're harassing me at home at this hour?'

Pasquano was appreciative.

'Because things are not what they seem.'

'Meaning?'

'For one, the dead man's one of us.'

'Oh.'

'And secondly, in my opinion, he was murdered. I've only done a superficial examination, mind you; I haven't opened him up yet.'

'Find any gunshot wounds?'

'No.'

'Stab wounds?'

'No.'

'Atom-bomb wounds?' asked Montalbano, losing

patience. 'What is this, Doc, a quiz? Would you just come out with it?'

'Come by tomorrow morning, and my illustrious colleague Mistretta, who'll be performing the post-mortem, will give you my opinion – which he doesn't share, mind you.'

'Mistretta? Why, won't you be there?'

'No, I won't. I'm leaving tomorrow morning to see my sister, who's not doing so well.'

Montalbano now understood why Pasquano had phoned him. As a gesture of courtesy and friendship. The doctor knew how much Montalbano detested Dr Mistretta, an arrogant, presumptuous man.

'As I was saying,' Pasquano went on, 'Mistretta doesn't agree with me about the case, and I wanted to tell you in private what I thought.'

'I'll be right over.'

'Where?'

'Over there, to your office.'

'I'm not at my office, I'm at home. We're packing our bags.'

'Then I'll come to your place.'

'No, it's too messy here. Listen, let's meet at the first bar on Viale Libertà, OK? But don't make me waste too much time, because I have to get up early tomorrow.'

✱

He got rid of Fazio, who had grown curious and demanded to know more, then quickly washed up, got in his car, and headed off to Montelusa. The first bar on Viale Libertà tended towards the squalid. Montalbano had been there only once, and that was more than enough. He went inside and immediately spotted Pasquano sitting at a table.

He sat down beside him.

'What'll you have?' asked Pasquano, who was drinking an espresso.

'Same as you.'

They sat there in silence until the waiter arrived with the second demi-tasse.

'So?' Montalbano began.

'You saw the shape the corpse was in?'

'Well, as I was towing it I was afraid his arm would fall off.'

'If you'd dragged it any further, it would have,' said Pasquano. 'The poor bastard had been in the water for over a month.'

'So he probably died some time last month?'

'More or less. Given the state of the body, it's hard for me to—'

'Did it still have any distinguishing marks?'

'He'd been shot.'

'So why did you tell me there weren't—'

'Would you let me finish, Montalbano? He had an old gunshot wound in his left leg. The bullet had splintered the bone. It must have happened a few years ago. I only noticed it because the salt water had eaten the flesh off the bone. He probably had a slight limp.'

'How old do you think he was?'

'About forty. And definitely not a non-European. He will, however, be hard to identify.'

'No fingerprints?'

'Are you kidding?'

'Doctor, why are you so convinced he was murdered?'

'It's just my opinion, mind you. The body's covered with wounds from having been dashed repeatedly against the rocks.'

'There aren't any rocks in the water where I found him.'

'How do you know where he's from? He'd been sailing a long time before turning himself over to you. What's more, he's all eaten up by crabs; he still had two of them in his throat, dead … As I was saying, he's covered with asymmetrical wounds, all of them post-mortem. But there are four that *are* symmetrical, perfectly defined, and circular.'

'Where?'

'Around his wrists and his ankles.'

'That's what it was!' exclaimed Montalbano, jumping out of his chair.

Before falling asleep that afternoon, he'd remembered a detail he couldn't decipher: the arm, the bathing suit wrapped tightly around the wrist…

'It was a cut that went all the way around the left wrist,' the inspector said slowly.

'So you noticed it, too? He had the same thing around

the other wrist and the ankles as well. And that, to me, can mean only one thing . . .'

'He'd been tied up.'

'Exactly. But with what? With iron wire. Pulled so tight that it sawed into his flesh. If it had been rope or nylon, the wounds wouldn't have been so deep as to cut almost down to the bone. And we certainly wouldn't have found any trace of them. No, before they drowned him, they took the wire off. They wanted to make it look like a routine drowning.'

'Any chance we can get some forensic tests done on him?'

'Maybe. It all depends on Dr Mistretta. We'd have to order the tests specially from Palermo, to see if there are any traces of metal or rust remaining inside the cuts around the wrists and ankles. But it'd take a long time. And that's the long and the short of it. It's getting late.'

'Thanks for everything, Doctor.'

They shook hands. The inspector got back in his car and drove off at a leisurely pace, lost in thought. A car came up behind him and flashed its high beam, reproaching him for going so slowly. When Montalbano pulled over to the right, the other car, a kind of silver torpedo, passed and came to a sudden stop in front of him. Cursing, the inspector slammed on the brakes. In the beam of his headlights, he saw a hand emerge from the torpedo's window and give him the finger. Seething with rage, Montalbano got out of his car, ready to have it out with the driver. The torpedo's driver also got out. Montalbano stopped dead in his tracks. It was Ingrid, arms open and smiling.

'I recognized the car,' said the Swede.

How long had it been since they'd last seen each other? Surely at least a year. They embraced long and hard. Ingrid kissed him, then lightly pushed him away, holding him at arm's length to have a better look.

'I saw you naked on TV,' she said laughing. 'You're still a pretty nice hunk.'

'And you're more beautiful than ever,' said the inspector in all sincerity.

Ingrid embraced him again.

'Is Livia here?'

'No.'

'Then I'd like to come sit a while on your veranda.'

'OK.'

'Give me a second. I need to break an engagement.'

She murmured something into her mobile phone, then asked, 'Got any whisky?'

'A whole bottle, still unopened. Here, Ingrid, take my house keys. You go on ahead, I can't keep up with you.'

She laughed, took his keys, and had already vanished by the time the inspector turned on the ignition. He was pleased by this chance encounter. It would not only afford him the pleasure of spending a few hours with an old friend, but would grant him the distance necessary to think with a cool head about what Dr Pasquano had just revealed to him.

When he pulled up in front of his house, Ingrid came up to him, embraced him, and held him tight.

'I have authorization.'

'From whom?'

'From Livia. The minute I went inside, the phone started ringing, so I answered. I shouldn't have, I know, but it was an instinctive reaction. It was her. I told her you'd be home in a few minutes, but she said she wouldn't call back. She said you hadn't been feeling too well and that, as your nurse, I was authorized to comfort you and take care of you. And this is the only way I know how to comfort and take care of people.'

Shit. Livia must have been seriously upset. Ingrid hadn't understood, or had pretended not to understand, Livia's venomous irony.

'Excuse me just a minute,' said Montalbano, breaking free of her embrace.

He dialled Livia's number in Boccadasse, but it was busy. She'd taken the phone off the hook, no doubt about it. He tried again. Meanwhile Ingrid roamed about the house, digging up the whisky bottle, getting some ice cubes from the freezer, going out on the veranda, and sitting down. The line remained busy. The inspector gave up, went outside, and sat down next to Ingrid on the bench. It was an exquisite night. There were a few light, wispy clouds in the sky, and the waves washed ashore with a caressing hush. A thought – a question, really – came into the inspector's head and made him smile. Would the night have seemed so idyllic if Ingrid hadn't been there beside him, head resting on his shoulder after having poured him a generous dose of whisky?

Then Ingrid started talking about herself and didn't finish until three and a half hours later, when only four fingers of whisky remained in the bottle before it could be officially declared dead. She said her husband was acting like the arsehole he was and that they lived separate lives under one roof; she said she'd gone to Sweden because she'd felt a longing for her family ('You Sicilians gave me the bug'); and she admitted she'd had two affairs. The first was with a member of Parliament, a strict Catholic who went by the name of Frisella or Grisella – the inspector couldn't quite hear which – and who before getting into bed with her would kneel on the floor and beg God's forgiveness for the sin he was about to commit. The second was with the captain of an oil tanker who'd taken early retirement after coming into a generous inheritance, and it could have become a serious involvement if she hadn't decided to call things off. This man, who went by the name of D'Iunio or D'Ionio – the inspector couldn't quite hear which – troubled her and made her feel uncomfortable. Ingrid had an extraordinary ability to grasp at once the comical or grotesque aspects of her men, and this amused Montalbano. It was a relaxing evening, better than a massage.

✶

Next morning, despite an eternal shower and four cups of coffee, gulped down one after the other, when he got into his car his head was still numb from the whisky. As for everything else, he felt entirely back on track.

'J'you get over your illment, Chief?' asked Catarella as the inspector walked into headquarters.

'My illment's a lot better, thanks.'

'Hey, I saw you on TV, Chief. Jesus, what an embodiment you got!'

The inspector went into his office and called Fazio, who arrived in a flash. The sergeant was dying to know what Dr Pasquano had told him, but didn't dare ask. He didn't open his mouth at all, in fact, because he was keenly aware that these were dark days for the inspector, and the slightest peep might set him off. Montalbano waited for him to sit down, pretending to look at some papers out of sheer meanness, since he could clearly see Fazio's question etched in the curve of his lips. He wanted to let him stew a little. Then, all at once, without looking up from his papers, he said:

'Murder.'

Taken by surprise, Fazio jumped out of his chair.

'Shot?'

'Nuh-unh.'

'Stabbed?'

'Nuh-unh. Drowned.'

'But how did Dr Pasquano—'

'Pasquano merely took a look at the body and formed an opinion. But Pasquano's almost never wrong.'

'And what's he base his opinion on?'

The inspector told him everything. And he added:

'The fact that Mistretta doesn't agree with Pasquano actually helps us. In his report, under the heading "Cause of Death", Mistretta will surely write: "Drowning", using the proper forensic terminology, of course. And that'll be our cover. We can work in peace without any interference from the commissioner's office, the flying squad, or anyone else.'

'What do you want me to do?'

'First of all, you should request an identification profile for the victim: height, hair colour, age, things like that.'

'And a photo, too.'

'Fazio, didn't you see the state he was in? Did that look like a face to you?'

Fazio looked crestfallen.

'If it'll make you feel any better,' the inspector continued, 'I can tell you that he probably limped. He'd been shot in the leg some time ago.'

'It's still going to be tough to identify him.'

'Try anyway. Have a look at the disappearance reports, too. Pasquano says the body'd been cruising the seas for at least a month.'

'I'll try,' said Fazio, unconvinced.

'I'm going out. I'll be back in a couple of hours.'

*

He headed straight for the port, stopped the car, got out, and walked towards a wharf where two fishing boats were moored, the rest having already gone out to sea some time before. Luckily, the *Madre di Dio* was there, having its motor overhauled. He approached and saw the captain and owner, Ciccio Albanese, standing on deck, overseeing operations.

'Ciccio!'

'Is that you, Inspector? I'll be right down.'

They'd known each other a long time and were fond of one another. Albanese was a brine-bitten sixty-year-old who'd been working on fishing boats since the age of six and who people said had no peer when it came to knowing the sea between Vigàta and Malta and all the way to Tunisia. He could find mistakes in nautical charts and navigation manuals. It was whispered about town that when work was scarce, he wasn't above smuggling cigarettes.

'Is this a good time, Ciccio?'

'Absolutely, Inspector. For you, I'm always available.'

Montalbano explained what he wanted from him. Albanese limited himself to asking how much time it would take, and the inspector told him.

46

'I'll be back in a couple of hours, boys.'

He followed behind Montalbano, who was heading towards his car. They rode in silence. The guard at the morgue told the inspector that Dr Mistretta wasn't in yet; only Jacopello, his assistant, was there. Montalbano felt relieved. Meeting with Mistretta would have ruined the rest of his day. Jacopello was quite loyal to Pasquano, and his face lit up when he saw the inspector.

'Good to see you!'

With Jacopello, the inspector knew he could lay his cards on the table.

'This is my friend, Ciccio Albanese. He's a man of the sea. If Mistretta'd been here, we'd have told him my friend wanted to see the body, fearing it might be one of his deck hands gone overboard. But there's no need to act with you. If Mistretta asks you any questions when he comes in, you know what to answer. Right?'

'Right. Follow me.'

The corpse, in the meantime, had grown even paler. It looked like a skeleton with an onion skin laid over it and bits of flesh randomly attached here and there. As Albanese was examining it, Montalbano asked Jacopello:

'Do you know how Dr Pasquano thinks this poor bastard was killed?'

'Of course. I was there for the discussion. Mistretta's wrong. See for yourself.'

The deep, circular grooves around the wrists and ankles had turned greyish.

'Jacopè, think you could persuade Mistretta to order that test Pasquano wanted done on the tissues?'

Jacopello laughed.

'Want to bet I can?'

'Make a bet with you? Never.'

Jacopello was a well-known betting enthusiast. He made bets with everyone on everything from the weather forecast to how many people would die of natural causes over the course of a week, and he rarely lost.

'I'll think up some reason to convince him that we're better off having that analysis done. How are we going to look if Inspector Montalbano later discovers that the guy didn't die by accident, but was murdered? Mistretta will sacrifice his arse if he has to, but he doesn't like to lose face. But I'm warning you, Inspector, those tests take a long time.'

Only during the drive back did Albanese decide to emerge from his silence.

'Bah,' he managed to mutter.

'What?' the inspector said in vexation. 'You look at a dead body for half an hour and all you can say is "bah"?'

'It's all very strange,' said Albanese. 'And I've certainly seen my share of drowning victims. But this one—' he interrupted himself to follow another thought: 'How long did the doctor say he'd been in the water?'

'A good month.'

'No, Inspector. Two good months, at least.'

'But after two months in the water, there wouldn't have been any body left, just pieces here and there.'

'That's what's so strange about it.'

'Explain, Ciccio.'

'The fact is that I don't like to talk bullshit.'

'If you only knew how much comes out of my mouth! Come on, Ciccio, out with it!'

'You saw the wounds made by the rocks, right?'

'Right.'

'They're superficial, Inspector. This past month we had rough seas for ten days straight. If the body was thrown against any rocks in those waters, it wouldn't have that kind of wound. It would have had its head knocked off, or some ribs broken, or a few bones sticking out.'

'So? Maybe during those bad days you mention, the body was out on the open sea, far from any rocks.'

'But Inspector, you found it in an area where the currents go backwards!'

'What do you mean?'

'Didn't you find it right off Marinella?'

'Yes.'

'Well, the currents there either go out to sea or run parallel to the coast. Another two days and the body would have passed Capo Russello, you can be sure of that.'

Montalbano fell silent, lost in thought. Then he said:

'You'll have to explain this business about the currents a little better for me.'

'Whenever you like.'

'You free tonight?'

'Yessir. Why don't you come to my place for dinner? My wife's making striped surmullet her own special way.'

Immediately Montalbano's tongue was drowning in saliva.

'Thanks. But what do you make of all this, Ciccio?'

'Can I speak freely? First of all, rocks don't leave the kind of wounds that guy had around his wrists and ankles.'

'Right.'

'He must have been tied up by the wrists and ankles before they drowned him.'

'With iron wire, according to Pasquano.'

'Right. Then they took the body and let it soak for a while in sea water, probably in some secluded place. Then, when they figured he was pretty well pickled, they put 'im out to sea.'

'Why would they wait so long?'

'Inspector, those guys wanted to make it look like the body came from far away.'

Montalbano looked at him with admiration. Not only had Ciccio Albanese, a man of the sea, come to the same conclusions as Dr Pasquano, a man of science, and Montalbano, a man of iron-clad police logic; he also had taken a big step forward.

FOUR

But the inspector was destined never to get so much as a whiff, not even from afar, of the striped surmullets specially prepared by Ciccio Albanese's wife. Around eight that evening, when he was getting ready to leave the office, a call came in for him from Deputy Commissioner Riguccio. Though he'd known him for years and they got on rather well, their relationship had never gone beyond the confines of work. It wouldn't have taken much for it to turn into friendship, but neither of them could make up his mind.

'Hello, Montalbano? Sorry, but is there anyone in your office who wears glasses with a correction of three for short-sightedness in both eyes?'

'Huh?' the inspector replied. 'We've got two patrolmen who wear glasses, Cusumano and Torretta, but I have no idea what their prescriptions are. Why do you ask? Is this some survey you're doing for your beloved minister?'

It was no mystery that Riguccio's political positions were close to those of the new government.

'I haven't got time for jokes, Salvo. See if they've got a pair that might work for me and send them over to me as soon as possible. Mine just broke and I'm lost without my glasses.'

'Don't you have an extra pair at the office?' asked Montalbano as he was calling Fazio.

'I do, but I'm not in Montelusa.'

'Where are you?'

'Here in Vigàta. On tourist duty.'

The inspector explained the problem to Fazio.

'Riguccio? I'm having somebody look into it. How many tourists you got today?'

'At least a hundred and fifty, on two of our patrol craft. They came across on two big boats that were shipping water and about to crash into the rocks at Lampedusa. From what I could gather, their guides abandoned them at sea and escaped on a dinghy. They were all about to drown, poor things. You know something, Montalbà? I don't think I can stand to see any more of these wretched people. They—'

'Tell it to your pals in the government.'

Fazio came back with a pair of glasses.

'The left eye's a three, the right eye, two and a half.'

Montalbano passed this information on.

'Perfect,' said Riguccio. 'Could you send them over to me? The patrol boats are docking right now.'

For whatever reason, Montalbano decided to take them himself, personally in person, as Catarella would say. All things considered, Riguccio was an excellent fellow, and it wasn't the end of the world if the inspector got to Ciccio Albanese's house a little late.

He was happy not to be in Riguccio's shoes. The Montelusa commissioner's office had asked the harbour authority that they be informed every time a new group of illegal immigrants arrived, and whenever this happened, Riguccio would head off to Vigàta with the requisite convoy of buses, police vans full of policemen, ambulances, and Jeeps, and was greeted every time by the same scenes of tragedy, tears, and sorrow. There were women giving birth, children lost in the confusion, people who'd lost their wits or fallen ill during endless journeys outside on the deck, exposed to the wind and the rain, and they all needed help. When they disembarked, the fresh sea air wasn't enough to dispel the unbearable stench they carried with them, which was a smell not of unwashed bodies but of fear, anguish, and suffering, of despair that had reached the point beyond which lies only the hope of death. It was impossible to remain indifferent to all this, and that was why Riguccio had admitted he couldn't stand it any longer.

When he got to the port, the inspector noticed that the first patrol boat had already lowered its gangplank. The policemen had lined up in two parallel rows, forming a kind of human corridor all the way to the first bus, which was waiting with its motor running. Standing at the bottom of the gangplank, Riguccio thanked Montalbano and put the glasses on. The inspector got the impression his colleague was so intent on supervising the situation that he hadn't even recognized him.

Riguccio then gave the signal to begin the disembarkation. The first person to come out was a black woman with a belly so big she looked like she might give birth at any moment. She was unable to walk on her own. A sailor from the patrol boat and a black man helped her along. When they got to the ambulance, there was some shouting when the black man wanted to get in with the woman. The sailor tried to explain to the police that the man was surely her husband, since he'd had his arms around her the whole time on the boat. Nothing doing, it couldn't be allowed. The ambulance pulled away with its siren wailing. The black man started crying, and the sailor took his arm, accompanying him to the bus and talking to him all the while. Feeling curious, the inspector approached them. The sailor was speaking a dialect; he must have hailed from Venice or somewhere thereabouts, and the black man didn't understand a thing, but clearly felt comforted by the friendly sound of the sailor's words.

Montalbano had just decided to go back to his car when he saw a group of four refugees stumble and stagger as though drunk when they reached the end of the gangplank. For a moment he didn't understand what was happening. Then he saw a small boy, not more than six years old, dart out between the legs of the four men. But the child disappeared as suddenly as he had appeared,

passing through the formation of policemen in the twinkling of an eye. As two officers began to give chase,
Montalbano saw the kid heading, with the instinct of a
hunted animal, towards the less lighted area of the wharf,
where stood the remains of an old silo that had been ringed
by a wall for security. He never knew what made him shout
to the two policemen:

'Stop! I'm Inspector Montalbano! Turn back! I'll go
after him myself!'

The policemen obeyed.

By now the inspector had lost sight of the kid, but the
direction he'd taken could only have led him to one place,
and that was an enclosed area, a kind of blind alley between
the back of the old silo and the boundary wall of the port,
which offered no path of escape. The space, moreover,
was cluttered with empty jerry cans and bottles, hundreds
of broken fish crates, and at least two or three scrapped
outboard motors from fishing boats. It was hard enough
to make one's way through that jumble in the daytime,
let alone by the faint glow of a street lamp. Certain that
the kid was watching him, he assumed a falsely casual air,
walking slowly, one step at a time. He even lit a cigarette.
When he'd reached the entrance to the alley, he called out
in a soft, calm voice:

'Come out, little boy, I'm not going to harm you.'

No answer. But, listening very hard, he could distinctly
hear, under the tide of shouts, wails, curses, car horns,

sirens, and screeching tyres that reached his ears from the wharf, the faint, panting breath of the little boy, who must have been hiding just a few yards away.

'Come on out now, I'm not going to harm you.'

He heard some rustling. It came from a wooden crate right in front of him. The boy must have been huddled behind it. He could have leapt forward and nabbed him, but chose to keep still. Then he saw the hands, arms, head, and chest slowly appear. The rest of the little body remained hidden by the crate. The boy was holding his hands up, signalling surrender, eyes open wide in terror. But he was trying very hard not to cry, not to show any weakness.

What corner of hell could he have come from, Montalbano suddenly asked himself in dismay, if at his age he'd already learned the terrible gesture of throwing one's hands in the air, something he certainly hadn't seen on television or at the movies?

The answer came to him at once, in the form of a flash in his brain. And while it lasted, inside this flash – which was just like a photographer's flash – the crate, the alley, the port, Vigàta itself all disappeared and then reappeared in black and white and shrunken to the size of an old photo he had seen many years before but which had been taken many years before that, during the war, before he was born, and which showed a little Jewish or Polish boy with hands raised and the very same wide-open eyes, the very same desire not to cry, as a soldier pointed a gun at him.

The inspector felt a sharp pain in his chest, a twinge that took his breath away. Frightened, he closed his eyes tight, then reopened them. Finally, everything returned to normal size, to the light of reality, and the little boy was no longer Jewish or Polish but a little black boy again. Montalbano took a step forward, took the child's freezing hands in his own and held them tight. And he remained that way, waiting for a little of his own warmth to pass into those tiny fingers. Only when he felt the little hands begin to relax did he take his first step, still holding him by one hand. The little boy followed, willingly entrusting himself to his care. In spite of himself, the inspector thought of François, the Tunisian boy who could have become his son, if Livia had had her way. He managed in time to suppress his emotion, biting his lower lip until it almost bled.

The disembarkation continued. In the distance he saw a rather diminutive woman making a scene with two small children hanging on her skirts. She was shouting incomprehensibly, pulling her hair out, stamping her feet, tearing her blouse. Three policemen tried to calm her down, with little success. Then the woman spotted the inspector and the little boy, and there was no stopping her: she shoved the policemen aside with all her might and rushed towards the two of them with her arms out. At that moment two things happened. First, Montalbano distinctly noticed that upon seeing his mother, the boy stiffened, ready to run away again. Why did he do this instead of running to meet her? Montalbano turned to him and was astonished to see that the boy was looking at him, not at his mother, with a desperate, questioning look in his eyes. Maybe he wanted to be left free to escape because his mother was sure to beat him for running away in the first place. The second thing was that, as she was running, the mother turned her ankle and fell to the ground. The three policemen tried to get her back on her feet but were unable. She couldn't stand up. She was wailing and touching her left knee, and meanwhile kept gesturing to the inspector to bring the boy to her. As soon as the boy was within reach, she embraced him and overwhelmed him with kisses. But she still couldn't manage to stand up. She tried repeatedly, but kept falling back down. Finally someone called an ambulance. Two medics stepped out, and one of them, a very thin man with a moustache, bent over the woman and touched her leg.

'She must have broken it,' he said.

They loaded her into the ambulance with her three children and left. By now the refugees from the second patrol boat were starting to disembark, but the inspector had already decided to go home to Marinella. He looked at his watch: it was almost ten. No point going to Ciccio Albanese's house. So much for the striped surmullets. By now they were no longer waiting for him. Anyway, he no longer felt hungry. His stomach was tied in a knot.

As soon as he got home he called Ciccio. The captain

said they'd waited a long time for him, but realized in the end that he wasn't coming.

'I'm still available to explain that stuff about the currents,' he said.

'Thanks, Ciccio.'

'If you want, I could come by the station in the morning, since I won't be taking the boat out tomorrow. I'll bring along my charts.'

'OK.'

*

He stayed in the shower a long time, to wash away all the things he had seen. He could feel them inside him, reduced to invisible fragments that had entered through his pores. He put on the first pair of trousers that came within reach and went into the living room to call Livia. As he reached for the phone, it rang all by itself. He jerked his hand back, as if he'd touched fire. An instinctive, unchecked reaction, which showed that, despite the shower, the thought of what he had seen on the wharf was still churning inside him and making him edgy.

'Hello, darling. Are you OK?'

All at once he felt the need to have Livia there beside him, so he could embrace her and be comforted by her. But since he was the way he was, he answered only:

'Yes.'

'Over your cold?'

'Yes.'

'Completely?'

He should have realized that Livia was setting him up, but he was too nervous and had other things on his mind.

'Completely.'

'So Ingrid must have taken good care of you. Tell me what she did for you. Did she put you to bed? Did she tuck in the sheets? Did she sing you a lullaby?'

Like a fool, he'd stepped right into the trap. All he could do now was counter-attack.

'Listen, Livia, I've had a very trying day. I'm extremely tired and have no desire to—'

'So you're really, really tired?'

'Yes.'

'Why don't you call Ingrid and get her to perk you up?'

He would never win a war of aggression against Livia. Maybe he'd stand a better chance in a defensive war.

'Why don't you come down here yourself?'

He'd intended to use the question tactically, but had said it with such sincerity that Livia was caught off guard.

'Do you mean that?'

'Of course. What day is it today, Tuesday? OK, tomorrow, when you get to work, you ask for a little advance on your holiday. Then you hop on a plane and come down.'

'You know, I have half a mind to—'

'No halves about it.'

'Oh, Salvo, if only it was up to me ... We're very busy at the office these days. But I'll try anyway.'

'Among other things, I want to tell you about something that happened to me tonight.'

'Come on, tell me now.'

'No, I want to be able to look you in the eye when I tell you.'

They stayed on the line another half-hour, but wished they could talk even longer.

*

The phone call, however, had made him miss the Free Channel's late-night newscast.

He turned on the television anyway and tuned in to TeleVigàta.

The first thing they said was that as one hundred and fifty illegal immigrants were being put ashore in Vigàta, a tragedy had occurred in Scroglitti, in eastern Sicily, where a large boat crammed with would-be immigrants slammed into rocks in bad weather. Thus far fifteen bodies had been recovered.

'But the number of victims is expected to rise,' said a reporter, using what had unfortunately become a stock phrase.

Meanwhile they showed images of drowned corpses, arms dangling inert, heads thrown back, children wrapped in pointless blankets that could never warm their dead bodies again, relief workers with contorted faces, people running wildly to waiting ambulances, a kneeling priest praying. Upsetting stuff. But for whom? the inspector asked himself. The more one saw those kinds of images – so different yet so similar – the more one got used to them. One looked at them, said 'poor things', and continued eating one's spaghetti with clam sauce.

After these images, the purse-lipped face of Pippo Ragonese appeared.

'In cases such as these,' said the channel's chief editorialist, 'it is absolutely imperative to appeal to cold reason and not let oneself be carried away by instinct and sentiment. We must consider a simple fact: our Christian civilization cannot allow itself to be altered at its very foundations by the uncontrollable hordes of desperate, lawless people who daily land on our shores. These people represent a genuine threat to us, to Italy, and to the entire Western world. The Cozzi–Pini law recently passed by our government is the only real bulwark we have against this invasion, no matter what the opposition says. But let's turn to a knowledgeable voice from Parliament, the honourable Cenzo Falpalà, and hear what he has to say on this pressing question.'

Falpalà was a man whose face expressed above all an effort to let the world know that nobody would ever pull a fast one on him.

'I have only a brief statement to make. The Cozzi–Pini law is proving that it works quite well. If immigrants are dying, this is precisely because the law provides us with the tools to prosecute the human traffickers who, at the first sign of trouble, have no qualms about throwing those desperate people overboard to avoid arrest. I would like, moreover, to say that—'

Montalbano suddenly got up and changed the channel, not so much enraged as disheartened by so much presumptuous stupidity. They were deluded to think they could stop a historic migration with police measures and laws. He remembered the time he noticed that the hinges on the main door of a church in a Tuscan town had been bent backwards by a force so strong as to push them in the opposite direction from the one in which they'd been designed to go. When he asked a man from the town to explain this, he was told that, during the war, the Nazis had put all the town's men inside the church, locked the door, and started throwing in hand grenades from above. The people inside, in their desperation, had forced the door to open in the opposite direction, and many had managed to escape.

Well, those people flooding in from all the poorest, most devastated parts of the world were strong enough and desperate enough to turn history's hinges back on themselves. And tough shit for Cozzi, Pini, Falpalà, and company, who were both the cause and the effect of a world filled with terrorists who could kill three thousand Americans in a single blow, with Americans who considered the thousands of civilians killed by their bombs 'collateral damage', with motorists who squashed pedestrians with their cars and never stopped to help them, with mothers who killed infants in their cradles for no reason at all, with children who slit the throats of mothers, fathers, brothers, and sisters for money, with fraudulent balance sheets that according to new rules were no longer considered fraudulent, with people who should have been thrown in jail years ago but who were not only free but rewriting the rules and dictating the law.

To distract himself and calm his nerves a little, he channel-surfed for a while until he came to a station showing two very swift yachts racing neck-and-neck in a regatta.

'This long-awaited, fierce, but highly sporting contest between the *Stardust* and the *Brigadoon*, permanent rivals, is about to draw to a close. Yet we still can't say which will emerge as the winner of this magnificent competition. The upcoming turn at the buoy will surely be decisive.'

There was a panning shot from a helicopter above. A dozen other boats straggled behind the two in the lead.

'We're at the buoy!' the announcer yelled.

The first boat went into its manoeuvre, elegantly putting about and rounding the mark as closely as possible before heading back the same way it had come.

'But what's happening to the *Stardust*?' asked the announcer, upset. 'Something's not right.'

Strangely, the *Stardust* had made no sign of any manoeuvre, but just charged on straight ahead, even faster than before, riding a stiff following wind. There was no getting around it. Was it possible the crew never even saw the buoy? Then something unheard of happened. Apparently out of control — maybe the rudder was stuck — the *Stardust* went and rammed straight into a kind of trawler sitting motionless in its path.

'Unbelievable! She just rammed the officials' boat broadside! The two vessels are starting to sink! Here comes help! Unbelievable! It looks like nobody's hurt. Believe me, friends, in all my years covering sailing competitions, I have never seen anything like it!'

Here the commentator started laughing. And Montalbano laughed, too, as he turned off the TV.

✳

He slept poorly, drifting off into short dreams from which he woke up in a daze every time. One of these dreams struck him in particular. He was with Dr Pasquano, who had to perform a post-mortem on an octopus.

Nobody seemed surprised by this. Pasquano and his assistants treated the matter like business as usual. Only Montalbano found the situation odd.

'Excuse me, Doctor,' he said, 'but since when have we been doing autopsies on octopuses?'

'Don't you know? It's a new directive from the Minister of Justice.'

'Oh. And, afterwards, what are you going to do with the remains?'

'They're going to be distributed to the poor, for them to eat.'

The inspector wasn't convinced.

'I don't understand the reasoning behind this directive.'

Pasquano gave him a long stare and then said:

'It's because things are not what they seem.'

Montalbano remembered that this was the same thing the doctor had said to him about the corpse he'd found in the water.

'Want to see?' asked Pasquano, brandishing the scalpel and then lowering it.

Suddenly the octopus turned into a child, a little black boy. Dead, of course, but with his eyes still wide open.

*

As he was shaving, the scenes of the previous evening on the wharf ran through his head again. Little by little, as he reviewed them with a cold eye, he began to feel uneasy, disturbed. There was something that didn't jibe, some detail that clashed with the rest.

He stubbornly played the scenes over in his head, trying to bring them more into focus. No dice. He lost heart. This was surely a sign of ageing. He used to be able to find the flaw, the jarring note in the overall picture, without fail.

Better not to think about it.

FIVE

As soon as he entered his office, he summoned Fazio.

'Any news?'

Fazio looked surprised.

'Chief, there hasn't been enough time. I'm still working on the preliminaries. I've checked the missing persons reports, of course, both here and in Montelusa—'

'Well done!' the inspector said snidely.

'Why are you mocking me, Chief?'

'You think that corpse was out for an early morning swim and heading home?'

'No, but I had to check things out here, too. Then I asked around, but it looks like nobody knew him.'

'Did you get an ID profile on him?'

'Yessir. About forty years old, five foot eight and a half, black hair, brown eyes. Stocky build. Distinguishing marks: an old scar on the left leg, just under the knee. He probably limped. And that's it.'

'Nothing to get excited about.'

'Yeah. That's why I decided to do something.'

'What'd you do?'

'Well, considering that you're not too fond of Dr Arquà, I went to Forensics and asked a friend for a favour.'

'And what was that?'

'I asked if he could make me a computerized sketch of what the guy might have looked like before he died. It should be ready by tonight.'

'Listen, I never ask Arquà for any favours, not even if you put a knife to my throat.'

'Don't worry, Chief. It'll remain between me and my friend.'

'What do you intend to do in the meantime?'

'Hit the road. I've got a few things to take care of first, but then I'm going to take my own car and check out the towns along the coast, both to the west and to the east. I'll contact you the minute I have any news.'

As soon as Fazio left, the door flew open and slammed violently against the wall. Montalbano, however, didn't move; he knew it was Catarella. By now he was used to these entries. What could he do? Shoot him? Keep the door to his office always open? All he could do was put up with it.

''Pologies, Chief. Hand slipped.'

'Come in, Cat.'

He said it with the exact same intonation as the De Rege brothers' legendary 'Come in, cretin.'

'Chief, seeing as how a journalist phoned this morning

asking for you, I jes' wanted to let you know that he said he was gonna call you back.'

'Did he tell you his name?'

'Pontius Pilate, Chief.'

Was it too much to expect Catarella ever to get anybody's name right?

'Listen, Cat, when Mr Pilate calls back, tell him I'm in an urgent meeting with Caiaphas, at the Sanhedrin.'

'D'jou say Caiaphas, Chief? I sure won't forget that!'

But he remained standing in the doorway.

'Something wrong, Cat?'

'Lass nite I seen you on TV, Chief.'

'What do you do, Cat, spend all your free time watching me on TV?'

'No, Chief, it was by accidint.'

'What was it, a replay of me naked? I must be getting good ratings!'

'No sir, you was drissed. I seen you past midnight on the Free Channel. You was on the docks, tellin' two of our men to go back 'cause you could take care of things y'self. Man, what a thorty you got!'

'OK, Cat, thanks. You can go now.'

He felt rather worried about Catarella. Not because he had any doubts about his sexuality, but because if he, the inspector, resigned — as he'd already decided to do — surely Catarella would suffer terribly, like a dog abandoned by its master.

*

Ciccio Albanese showed up around eleven thirty, empty-handed.

'You didn't bring the charts you mentioned?'

'If I showed them to you, would you understand them?'

'No.'

'So why should I bring them? It's better if I explain things myself.'

'Tell me something, Ciccio. Do all of you trawler captains use maps?'

Albanese looked at him cockeyed.

'Are you kidding? In our line of work, we know our stretch of sea by heart. Some of it we learned from our dads, some of it we learned by ourselves. For the new stuff, we get some help from radar. But the sea's always the sea.'

'So why do you use maps?'

'I don't, Inspector. I look at 'em and study 'em 'cause it's something I like to do. But I don't bring 'em aboard with me. I prefer to rely on experience.'

'So, what can you tell me?'

'First of all, I gotta tell you that before coming here this morning, I went to see *u zù Stefanu*.'

'I'm sorry, Ciccio, but I don't—'

'Stefano Lagùmina, but we all call him *u zù Stefanu*. He's ninety-five years old, but his brain's as sharp as anyone's. *U zù Stefanu* don't go out to sea any more, but he's the oldest fisherman in Vigàta. He used to have a lateener before he got a trawler. Whatever the man says is gospel.'

'So you wanted to consult with him.'

'Yessir. I wanted to make sure my hunch was right. And *u zù Stefanu* agrees with me.'

'And what are your conclusions?'

'Here's how I see it. The dead man was carried by a surface current that we all know well, and which runs east to west, always at the same speed. The spot off Marinella where you bumped into the body is where this current comes closest to shore. You follow?'

'Perfectly. Go on.'

'It's a slow current. You know how many knots?'

'No, and I don't want to know. And just between you and me, I don't even know how many knots there are in a mile.'

'Well, a mile's one thousand eight hundred and fifty-one point eighty-five metres long. An Italian mile, that is. 'Cause in England—'

'Forget about it, Ciccio.'

'Whatever you say, Inspector. As I was saying, this current comes from far away. It's not native. To give you an idea, we run into it way down at Capo Passero. That's where it enters our waters, and then it hugs the coast up to Mazara. After that it goes its own way.'

And there you have it! This, of course, meant that the body could have been thrown into the sea at just about any point along the southern coast of Sicily! Albanese read the discouragement on the inspector's face and came to his aid.

'I know what you're thinking. But I have something important to tell you. A little before Bianconara, this current is cut off by another, stronger current going in the opposite direction. And so a body floating from Pachino over to Marinella would never actually get to Marinella because the second current would carry it into the Gulf of Fela.'

'So that means that my dead body's story definitely begins after Bianconara.'

'Exactly, Inspector. You've understood everything.'

Thus the likely area of investigation was reduced to some forty miles of coastline.

'And I now should tell you,' Albanese continued, 'that I also talked to *u zù Stefanu* about the condition the body was in when you found it. I could see for myself: the man'd been dead at least two months. You agree?'

'Yes.'

'So I say: a corpse isn't going to take two months to float from Bianconara to Marinella. Maybe ten, fifteen days, at the most, if you figure in the speed of the currents and all.'

'And so?'

Ciccio Albanese stood up and held his hand out to Montalbano.

'That kind of question's not for me to answer. I'm only a sailor. That's where you come in, Inspector.'

A perfect assignation of roles. Ciccio didn't want to venture into waters not his own. All Montalbano could do was thank him and accompany him to the door. After the captain left, the inspector called Fazio.

'Have you got a map of the province?'

'I'll find one.'

After Fazio brought him one, he looked at it a moment and said:

'By way of consolation, I can tell you that, based on the information given me by Ciccio Albanese, the dead man you need to identify definitely hung out somewhere between Bianconara and Marinella.'

Fazio gave him a confused look.

'So?'

The inspector took offence.

'What do you mean, "So"? That greatly reduces the area we need to investigate!'

'Chief, everybody and his dog knows that the current starts at Bianconara! You don't think I was gonna go all the way to Fela to start asking questions!'

'OK, OK. The fact remains that we now know there are only five towns you have to visit.'

'Five?'

'Yes, five! You can look at the map and count them yourself.'

'Chief, there's eight towns in all. On top of the five, you have to add Spigonella, Tricase, and Bellavista.'

Montalbano looked down at the map, then looked up again.

'This map's from last year. How come they're not on it?'

'They're unauthorized towns.'

'Unauthorized *towns*? There are probably no more than four houses—'

Fazio interrupted him, shaking his head.

'No, Chief. They're towns, really and truly. The owners of those houses pay property tax to the nearest municipality. They've got sewers, running water, electricity, and phone service. And every year they get a little bigger. Everybody knows those houses are never going to be torn down, because no politician wants to lose their votes. You know what I mean? So in the end they're granted amnesty and authorization and everybody ends up happy. And that's to say nothing of all the houses and cottages built on the beach! Four or five of them even have a kind of private entrance gate.'

'Get out of here!' Montalbano ordered, upset.

'Hey, Chief, it's not my fault,' said Fazio, going out.

*

Late that morning, the inspector received two phone calls that aggravated his bad mood. The first was from Livia, who said she hadn't been able to get an advance on her holiday time. The second was from Jacopello, Pasquano's assistant.

'Is that you, Inspector?' he said straight off.

'Yes, it's me,' said Montalbano, instinctively lowering his voice.

They were like two conspirators.

'Excuse me for talking this way, but I don't want any of my colleagues to hear. I wanted to let you know that Dr Mistretta moved the post-mortem up to this morning, and he's convinced that it was an accidental drowning. Which means that he won't request those tests that Dr Pasquano wanted done. I tried to persuade him to change his mind, but there was no way. If you'd made that bet with me, you'd have won.'

What now? How was he ever going to proceed officially? By ruling out murder, that dickhead Mistretta's report slammed the door on any possibility of investigation. And the inspector didn't even have a missing-persons report in hand. No cover at all. For the moment, that corpse was a *nuddru ammiscatu cu nenti* – a combination of nothing and naught. But, like the reader exhorted by Eliot in his lines on Phlebas, the drowned Phoenician in 'Death by Water', Montalbano would keep on thinking of that nameless corpse. It was a matter of honour, for it was the dead man himself who, one cold morning, had come looking for him.

*

It was now time to eat. OK, but where? The confirmation that the inspector's world was starting to go to the dogs had come barely a month after the G8 meetings, when, after a meal of considerable magnitude, Calogero, the owner-cook-waiter of the Trattoria San Calogero, had announced he was retiring, however reluctantly.

'You shitting me, Calò?'

'No, Inspector. As you know, I've had two bypasses and am seventy-three years old and counting. Doctor don't want me to work any more.'

'And what about me?' Montalbano had blurted out.

He had suddenly felt as unhappy as a character in a pulp novel, like the girl seduced and abandoned and kicked out of her home with the child of sin in her womb, or the young woman selling matches in the snow, or the orphan rummaging through rubbish for something to eat...

By way of reply, Calogero had thrown his hands up in despair. The terrible day had come when Calogero whispered:

'Don't come by tomorrow. I'm closed.'

They had embraced, practically weeping. And his Via Crucis had begun. Between restaurants, trattorias, and osterias, he'd tried half a dozen new places in the days that followed, but they were no great shakes. Not that you could say, in all honesty, that their food was bad. The fact was that they all lacked that indefinable touch that Calogero's dishes had. For a while he had opted to eat at home instead of going out. Adelina made him one meal a day, but this created a problem: if he ate that meal at midday, then in the evening he would have to make do with a little cheese and olives and salted sardines or salami; if, on the other hand, he ate it in the evening, that would mean that at midday he had made do with cheese, olives, salted sardines, or salami. In the long run, the situation became disheartening. He went out hunting again and found a good restaurant near Capo Russello. It was right on the beach, the dishes were civilized, and it didn't cost a great deal. The problem was that between driving there, eating, and driving back, it took three hours at the very least, and he didn't always have that kind of time.

*

That day he decided to try out a trattoria that Mimì had suggested.

'Have you eaten there?' Montalbano had asked him suspiciously, having a very low opinion of Mimì's palate.

'Actually, no, but a friend who's even a bigger pain in the arse than you spoke well of it.'

Since the trattoria, called Da Enzo, was in the uphill part of town, the inspector resigned himself to driving there. From the outside, the dining room looked like a corrugated sheet-metal construction; the kitchen must have been inside the house next to it. The whole thing had a temporary feeling about it, which Montalbano liked. He went in and sat down at an empty table. A thin man with blue eyes, about sixty years old, who'd been overseeing the activities of the two waiters, approached and planted himself in front of the inspector without a word of greeting. He was smiling.

Montalbano gave him a questioning look.

'I knew it,' the man said.

'You knew what?'

'That after all that running around, you would come here. I was waiting for you.'

Apparently word of his Calvary following the closing of his usual trattoria had spread across town.

'Well, here I am,' the inspector said drily.

They looked each other in the eye. The shoot-out at the OK Corral had begun. Enzo summoned a waiter.

'Set the table for Inspector Montalbano and keep an eye on the room. I'm going into the kitchen. I'll see to the inspector myself.'

The antipasto of salted octopus tasted as though it were made of condensed sea and melted the moment it entered his mouth. The pasta in squid ink could have held its own against Calogero's. And the mixed grill of mullet, sea bass, and gilthead had that heavenly taste the inspector feared he had lost for ever. Music began to play in his head, a kind of triumphal march. He stretched out blissfully in his chair and took a deep breath.

After a long and perilous journey over the sea, Odysseus had finally found his long-lost Ithaca.

*

Partially reconciled with life, he got in his car and headed towards the port. There was no point dropping in at the *càlia e simenza* shop, which was closed at that hour. He left his car on the wharf and started to walk along the jetty. He ran into the usual angler, who greeted him with a wave of the hand.

'They biting?'

'Not even if you pay them.'

When he reached the rock under the lighthouse, he sat down. He fired up a cigarette and savoured it. When he'd finished, he threw it into the sea. Jostled by the motion of the water, the butt grazed first the rock he was sitting on, then the rock behind it. An idea flashed into Montalbano's brain. If that had been a human body instead of a butt, that body would not have grazed those rocks, but bumped against them, even if not very hard. Just as Ciccio Albanese had said. Looking up, he saw his car on the wharf in the distance. He realized he'd left it in exactly the same spot where he'd stood with the little boy as his mother kicked up such a row that she broke her leg. He got up and headed back. He wanted to know how that whole business had turned out. The mother was surely in a hospital somewhere with her leg in a cast.

When he got back to the office, he immediately phoned Riguccio.

'Oh, God, Montalbano, I'm so embarrassed!'

'Why?'

'I still haven't returned those glasses. I'd completely forgotten about them! It's so chaotic here that—'

'Rigù, I wasn't calling about the glasses. I wanted to ask you something. What hospitals are the sick, the injured, and pregnant women taken to?'

'To any one of the three hospitals in Montelusa, or else to—'

'Wait, I'm only interested in the ones who were put ashore yesterday.'

'Give me a minute.'

Apparently Riguccio had to flip through some papers before he could answer.

'Here, at the San Gregorio.'

Montalbano informed Catarella he'd be out for an hour or so, got in his car, stopped at a cafe, bought three slabs of chocolate, and headed towards Montelusa. San Gregorio Hospital was outside the city, but easy to reach from Vigàta. It took him about twenty minutes. He parked, went inside, and asked for directions to the orthopaedic ward. He got in the lift, got off at the third floor, and spoke to the first nurse he saw.

He told her he was looking for a non-European immigrant who had broken her leg the previous evening while disembarking at Vigàta. To help identify her, he added that the woman had three small children with her. The nurse looked a bit surprised.

'Would you wait here? I'll go check.'

She returned about ten minutes later.

'Just as I thought. There aren't any non-European

women here for a broken leg. We do have one who broke her arm, however.'

'May I see her?'

'I'm sorry, but who are you?'

'Inspector Montalbano.'

The nurse looked him over and must have immediately decided that the man standing before her had the face of a policeman, because she said only:

'Please follow me.'

But the immigrant woman with the broken arm was not black; she looked merely like she had a tan. Secondly, she was pretty, slender, and very young.

'You see,' said Montalbano, slightly flustered, 'the fact is that yesterday evening, I saw an emergency medical crew take her away in the ambulance with my own eyes...'

'Why don't you try the emergency ward?'

Of course. The medic might have been mistaken when he diagnosed her with a fracture. Maybe the woman had only a sprain, and there'd been no need to hospitalize her.

In the emergency ward, none of the three men who'd been on duty the previous evening remembered seeing a black woman with a broken leg and three small kids.

'Who was the doctor on call?'

'Dr Mendolìa. But today's his day off.'

By dint of effort and cursing, he managed to get the doctor's phone number. Dr Mendolìa was courteous, but had not seen any non-European woman with a fractured leg. No, not even a sprain. So much for that.

Once out of the hospital square, he saw some parked ambulances. A few steps away stood some people in white smocks, talking. As he drew near, he immediately recognized the gaunt medic with the moustache. The man recognized him as well.

'Last night, weren't you—?'

'Yes. Inspector Montalbano's the name. Where did you take that woman with the three children, the one who'd broken her leg?'

'To A&E here. But I was wrong, her leg wasn't broken. In fact, she got out of the ambulance by herself, though it took some effort. I saw her go into A&E.'

'Why didn't you accompany her?'

'Inspector, we'd just received an emergency call from Scroglitti. There was a huge mess over there. Why, can't you find her?'

SIX

Seen in the light of day, Riguccio was pale and unshaven, with bags under his eyes. Montalbano got worried.

'Are you sick?'

'I'm tired. My men and I can't take it any more. Every night there's another boatload, every night another twenty to a hundred and fifty illegals. The commissioner's gone to Rome just to explain the situation and ask for more men. Good luck! He'll return with a lot of sweet promises. What do you want?'

When Montalbano told him about the disappearance of the black woman and her three kids, Riguccio didn't make a sound. He merely looked up from the papers piled up on his desk and stared at the inspector.

'Take your time, while you're at it,' the inspector blurted out.

'And in your opinion, what should I do?' Riguccio snapped back.

'Bah, I dunno, do a search, send out a bulletin . . .'

'Have you got something against these wretched people?'

'Me?!'

'Yeah, you. Seems to me you want to hound them.'

'Hound them? Me? You're the one who agrees with this government!'

'Not always. Sometimes yes, sometimes no. Listen, Montalbà: I'm someone who goes to church on Sunday because I believe in it. End of story. Now let me tell you how things went the other night, because it wasn't the first time. That woman, you see, took you all for a ride, you, the ambulance men—'

'You mean she faked that fall?'

'Oh yes. It was all an act. She wanted to go to A&E, where they can basically come and go as they please.'

'But why? Did she have something to hide?'

'Probably. In my opinion, she was part of some kind of family reunion outside the law.'

'What do you mean?'

'Her husband is almost certainly an illegal who nevertheless managed to find work on the local black market. And he probably summoned his family here, with the help of people who make money from this kind of thing. If the woman had gone through the proper procedures, she would have had to declare that her husband was an illegal immigrant in Italy. And with the new law they would have all been kicked out of the country. So they took a short cut.'

'I see,' said the inspector.

He pulled the three slabs of chocolate out of his jacket pocket and laid them on Riguccio's desk.

'I bought them for those little kids,' he muttered.

'I'll give them to my son,' said Riguccio, putting them in his pocket.

Montalbano gave him an uncomprehending look. He knew that his colleague, after six years of marriage, had given up hope of having a child. Riguccio understood what was going through his head.

'Teresa and I managed to adopt a little boy from Burundi. Oh, I almost forgot. Here are the glasses.'

*

Catarella was puttering away at the computer, but the moment he saw the inspector, he dropped everything and ran up to him.

'Ah, Chief, Chief!' he began.

'What were you doing at the computer?' Montalbano asked.

'Oh, that? I's workin onna idinnification Fazio axed me to do. Of the dead guy who was swimmin when you was swimmin.'

'Good. What did you want to tell me?'

Catarella got flustered and stared at his shoes.

'Well?' asked Montalbano.

'Beggin' pardon, Chief, I forgot.'

'That's all right, when it comes back to you—'

'It's back, Chief! Pontius Pilate called again! And so I

tol' him as how you tol' me to tell him that you's meeting with Mr Caiphas and Sam Hedrin, but he made as like he din't unnastand, and so he tol' me to tell you as how he got something he gotta tell you.'

'OK, Cat. If he calls back, tell him to tell you what he has to tell me, so you can tell me yourself.'

'Chief, sorry, but I'm curious 'bout something. Wasn't Pontius Pilate the guy?'

'What guy?'

'The guy that washed 'is hands inni olden days?'

'Yes.'

'So he was the ansister of this guy that called?'

'When he calls back, you can ask him yourself. Is Fazio around?'

'Yessir, Chief. Got back just now.'

'Send him to me.'

*

'Can I sit down?' asked Fazio. 'With all due respect, my feet are smoking from all the walking I've been doing. And I've only just started.'

He sat down, pulled a small stack of photographs out of his jacket pocket, and handed these to the inspector.

'My friend in forensics got them to me fast,' he said.

Montalbano looked at them. They showed the face of an ordinary forty-year-old, with long hair in one, a moustache in another, a crew cut in another, and so on. But they were all, well, totally anonymous, inert, not personalized by any light in the eyes.

'Still looks dead,' said the inspector.

'What did you expect, for them to bring him back to life?' snapped Fazio. 'That's the best they could do. Don't you remember the state of the guy's face? For me they'll be an enormous help. I gave Catarella copies for comparison with the photo archives, but it's going to be a long haul, a real pain in the neck.'

'I'm sure it will,' said Montalbano. 'But you seem a little on edge. Anything wrong?'

'What's wrong, Chief, is that the work I've been doing, and the work still left for me to do, might be all for nothing.'

'Why?'

'We've been searching the towns along the coast. But who's to say the man wasn't killed in some inland town, put in the boot of a car, driven to a beach, and dumped in the sea?'

'I don't think so. Usually when somebody is killed in the countryside or some inland town, they end up inside a well or buried at the bottom of a mountain ravine. In any case, what's to prevent us from first checking the towns along the coast?'

'My poor feet, Chief, that's what.'

✻

Before going to bed, he phoned Livia. She was miserable because she couldn't come to Vigàta. Montalbano wisely let her vent her feelings, occasionally clearing his throat to let her know he was listening. Then, without a break, she asked:

'So, what did you want to tell me?'

'Me?'

'Come on, Salvo. The other night you said you had something to tell me, but you preferred to wait until I got there. Since now I can't come, you have to tell me everything over the phone.'

Montalbano cursed his big mouth. If he'd had Livia right in front of him when telling her of the little boy who'd tried to escape on the wharf, he could have weighed his words, tone, and gestures appropriately, to keep Livia from getting too sad thinking about François. At the slightest change in her expression, he would have known how to steer the drift of the conversation. Over the phone, on the other hand . . . He tried a last-ditch defence.

'You know what? I really don't remember what I wanted to tell you.'

He immediately bit his tongue. That was a stupid thing to say. Even from six thousand miles away, Livia, over the phone line, could immediately tell when he was lying.

'Don't even try, Salvo. Come on, tell me.'

During the whole ten minutes he spoke, Montalbano felt like he was walking through a minefield. Livia did not interrupt him once, and made no comment whatsoever.

'...And so my colleague Riguccio's convinced it was all for some kind of family reunion, as he calls it, and a successful one,' he concluded, wiping the sweat from his brow.

Not even the happy ending got a reaction from Livia. The inspector was worried.

'Livia. Are you still there?'

'Yes. I'm thinking.'

The tone was firm; her voice hadn't cracked.

'About what? There's nothing to think about. It's just a little story like any other, of no importance whatsoever.'

'Stop talking nonsense. I also understand why you would have preferred to tell me face to face.'

'Come on, what kind of ideas are you getting in your head? I didn't—'

'Never mind.'

Montalbano didn't breathe.

'Of course, it *is* strange,' Livia said a moment later.

'What is?'

'Does it seem normal to you?'

'If you don't tell me what you're talking about—'

'The boy's behaviour.'

'It seemed strange to you?'

'Of course. Why did he try to run away?'

'Try to imagine the situation, Livia! That child was in a panic.'

'I don't think so.'

'Why?'

'Because if a child in a panic has his mother beside him, he's going to grab her skirts and hang on with all his might, as you said the other two kids were doing.'

That's true, Montalbano said to himself.

'When he surrendered,' Livia continued, 'he didn't surrender to the enemy – which was you at that moment – but to the circumstances. He was lucid enough to realize there was no escape. It was the exact opposite of panic.'

'Tell me something,' said Montalbano. 'Are you telling me that boy was taking advantage of the situation to run away from his mother and siblings?'

'If things were the way you tell me, I would say so, yes.'

'But why would he do that?'

'That, I don't know. Maybe he wanted to go back to his father; that might be one logical explanation.'

'So he decides to run away in an unknown country where he can't speak the language, without a penny or a helping hand, with nothing at all? The kid was barely six years old!'

'Salvo, you'd be right if you were talking about one of us, but those kinds of children ... They may look six years old, but in terms of life experiences, they're like grown men. Between famine, war, massacres, death, and fear, you grow up fast.'

That's also true, Montalbano said to himself.

*

He lifted the sheet with one hand, leaned on the bed with the other, raised his left leg, and froze. A chill ran down his spine. It all came back to him at once: the look the little boy had given him as his mother ran up to take him back. At the time, he hadn't understood that look. Now, after talking to Livia, he did. The little boy's eyes were imploring him. They were telling him: for pity's sake, let me go, let me escape. And now, as he was about to get into bed, he felt bitterly guilty for not immediately understanding the meaning of that look. He was slipping. It was hard to admit, but true. How could he not have realized that, to use Dr Pasquano's words, things were not what they seemed?

*

'Chief? There's a nurse from San Gregorio Hospital in Montelusa onna line...'

What was happening to Catarella? He'd said the hospital's name right!

'What's she want?'

'She wants to talk to you poissonally in poisson. Says her name is Agata Militello. Want me to put her on?'

'Yes.'

'Inspector Montalbano? My name is Agata Militello...' A miracle! That was really her name. What could be happening if Catarella got two names in a row right? '...I'm a nurse at San Gregorio. I was told you came here yesterday looking for information on a black woman with three small children and you couldn't find her. I saw that woman with the three children.'

'When?'

'Night before last. When they started bringing in the wounded from Scroglitti, the hospital called me and asked me to come in to work. It was my day off. I live right nearby, and I always walk to work. Anyway, as I was approaching the hospital, I saw this woman running towards me, dragging three little kids behind her. When she was almost right beside me, a car drove up and came to a sudden stop. The man at the wheel called to the woman, and when they'd all got in the car, he drove off again at high speed.'

'Listen, I'm going to ask you something that may sound strange, but please think hard before answering. Did you notice anything unusual?'

'In what sense?'

'Well, I don't know... By any chance, did the oldest boy try to run away before getting in the car?'

Agata Militello thought it over carefully.

'No, Inspector. The biggest boy got in first; his mother pushed him in. Then the other kids, then the woman last.'

'Did you manage to see the licence plate?'

'No. It didn't occur to me. There wasn't any reason.'

'Indeed. Thank you for calling.'

Her testimony brought the whole affair to a definitive close. Riguccio was right. It was some kind of family reunion. Even though the biggest kid had ideas of his own about that reunion, and didn't want to go.

*

The door slammed hard, Montalbano jumped out of his chair, and a piece of plaster fell, even though the wall had been redone less than a month before. Looking up, the inspector saw Catarella standing motionless in the doorway. This time he hadn't even bothered to say his hand had slipped. He had such a look about him that a triumphal march would have been the ideal background music.

'Well?' asked Montalbano.

Catarella puffed up his chest and let out an elephantine sort of blast. Mimì came running from the next room, alarmed.

'What's happening?'

'I found 'im. I idinnified 'im!' Catarella yelled, walking up to the desk and laying down an enlarged photo and a computer printout of the profile.

The big photo and the much smaller one in the upper left-hand corner of the profile seemed to be of the same man.

'Would somebody please explain?' said Mimì Augello.

'Certainly, 'Nspecter,' Catarella said proudly. 'This here big photoraph was givenna me by Fazio, and it shows the dead man 'at was swimmin the other day with the Chief. This one here's the one I idinnified myself. Have a look, Chief. Ain't they like two peas in a pod?'

Mimì circled around the desk, went behind Montalbano, and bent down to get a better look. Then he gave his verdict.

'Yeah, they look alike. But they're not the same person.'

'But, 'Nspector Augello, you gotta consider a consideration.'

'And what would that be?'

'That the big photoraph's not a photoraph but a photoraph of a drawing of a face the man mighta had when 'e died. 'S just a drawing. Ya gotta allow a little margin of era.'

Mimì walked out of the office, unconvinced.

'They're not the same person.'

Catarella threw up his hands and looked over at the inspector, leaving his fate up to him. The dust or the altar, that was the question. There was a certain resemblance, that much was undeniable. Might as well check it out. The man's name was Ernesto Errera, a fugitive from justice the last two years, with a whole slew of crimes to his credit, all committed in Cosenza and environs, ranging from breaking and entering to armed robbery. To save time, it was better not to follow procedure.

'Cat, go to Inspector Augello and ask him if we have any friends in the Cosenza Police Department.'

Catarella returned, opened his mouth, and said:

'Vattiato, Chief. 'At's his name.'

It really was his name. For the third time in a row,

Catarella had been on the mark. Was the end of the world nigh?

'Call Cosenza Police, ask for Vattiato, and let me talk to him.'

Their Cosenza colleague was a man with a nasty disposition. He proved true to form this time as well.

'What is it, Montalbano?'

'I may have found one of your fugitives, a certain Ernesto Errera.'

'Really? Don't tell me you've arrested him!'

Why was he so surprised? Montalbano smelt a rat and decided to play defensively.

'Are you kidding? At best, I may have found his corpse.'

'Go on! Errera died almost a year ago and was buried in the cemetery here. His wife wanted it that way.'

Montalbano felt upset by the embarrassment.

'But his case was never closed, dammit!'

'We issued a notice of his decease. It's not my fault if the people in the records office don't do their job.'

They both hung up at the same time, without saying goodbye. For a second he was tempted to call Catarella and make him pay for his humiliation by Vattiato. Then he thought better of it. How was it poor Catarella's fault? If anything, it was his own fault, for wanting to proceed and not letting Mimì persuade him to drop the whole thing. Immediately another thought made him wince. Would he have been able, a few years ago, to tell who was right and who was wrong? Would he have so blithely admitted the mistake? And wasn't this, too, a sign of maturity, or rather – to mince no words – of old age?

✻

'Chief? That would be Dr Latte with an *S* onna phone. Whaddo I do, put 'im on?'

'Of course.'

'Inspector Montalbano? How are you? The family doing all right?'

'I can't complain. What can I do for you?'

'The commissioner's just back from Rome and he's called a plenary session of the department for three o'clock tomorrow afternoon. Will you be there?'

'Naturally.'

'I communicated your request for a private meeting to the commissioner. He'll see you tomorrow afternoon, right after the department meeting.'

'Thank you, Dr Lattes.'

So that was that. Tomorrow he would tender his resignation. With a fond goodbye to, among others, the swimming dead guy, as Catarella called him.

✻

That evening, phoning from home, he told Livia about the nurse's testimony. By way of conclusion, just when the inspector thought he had reassured her completely, Livia let out a sigh full of doubt.

'I don't know,' she said.

'Jesus Christ!' snapped Montalbano. 'You really won't let go of it! You don't want to accept the obvious!'

'And you're too ready to accept it.'

'What's that supposed to mean?'

'It means that in the past, you would have checked out the veracity of that testimony.'

'In the past!' Montalbano fumed. What was he, old as the hills? Some kind of Methuselah? 'I haven't done any checks because, as I already said, the whole business is of no importance. And anyway—'

He broke off, the gears in his brain screeching to a sudden halt.

'And anyway?' Livia insisted.

What to do? Stall? Say the first idiocy that came into his head? Right! Livia would have caught on immediately. Better to tell the truth.

'Anyway, tomorrow I'm seeing the commissioner.'

'Oh.'

'I'm tendering my resignation.'

'Oh.'

A horrendous pause.

'Goodnight,' said Livia.

She hung up.

SEVEN

He woke up at the crack of dawn but remained in bed, eyes open and staring at the ceiling, which brightened ever so slowly with the sky. The faint light filtering through the window was clear and steady, not varying in intensity as when clouds were passing. It promised to be a beautiful day. So much the better. Bad weather wouldn't have helped matters. He would be firmer, more decisive, when explaining the reasons for his resignation to the commissioner. Resignation. The word brought to mind an episode when he'd first joined the police, before coming to Vigàta... Then he remembered the time when... And that other time when... All at once the inspector understood why all these memories were flooding his brain. They say that when someone is about to die, the most important moments of his life pass before him as in a film. Was the same thing happening to him? Deep down, did he consider resignation a kind of death? He roused himself, hearing the telephone ring. He glanced at the clock. Eight o'clock already, and he hadn't even noticed. Jesus, what a long film his life was! Worse than *Gone With The Wind*! He got up and answered the phone.

'Morning, Chief, it's Fazio. I'm about to go out and continue my search...' (Montalbano was about to tell him to drop it, but changed his mind) '... and since I found out you're meeting with the commissioner this afternoon, I prepared some papers for you to sign as well as some other stuff, and put them all on your desk.'

'Thanks, Fazio. Any news?'

'Nothing, Chief.'

Since he had to go to the commissioner's office in the early afternoon and wouldn't have time to come home to Marinella and change, he had to get dressed up. He slipped the tie in his pocket, however; he would put it on in due course. It really annoyed him to wear a slip knot around his neck first thing in the morning.

*

The stack of papers on his desk was in a precarious state of balance. If Catarella barged in and slammed the door, they would witness a replay of the Tower of Babel's collapse. He signed for over an hour without once looking up, then felt the need for a little rest. He decided to go outside and smoke a cigarette. Out on the pavement, he stuck his hand in his pocket, searching for cigarettes and matches. Nothing. He'd left them at home. In their place was the tie he'd selected, green with little red dots. He shoved it back in his pocket at once, looking around like a thief who'd just stolen a purse. Christ! How had such an ignoble tie found its way into his wardrobe? And why hadn't he noticed its colours when he put it in his pocket? He went back inside.

'Cat, see if there's anyone here who can lend me a tie,' he said as he passed him on the way to his office.

Catarella turned up five minutes later with three ties.

'Whose are they?'

'Torretta's.'

'The same guy who lent his glasses to Riguccio?'

'Yessir.'

He chose the one that least clashed with his grey suit. After another hour and a half of signing, he'd managed to finish the stack. He looked around for the briefcase in which he normally put his papers when he went to meetings. He turned his office upside down looking for it, cursing the saints, but to no avail.

'Catarella!'

'Your orders, Chief!'

'Have you by chance seen my briefcase?'

'No sir, Chief.'

He had almost certainly taken it home and left it there.

'See if anyone in the office—'

'Right away, Chief.'

He returned with two almost new briefcases, one black, the other brown. Montalbano chose the black.

'Where'd you get them?'

'Torretta, Chief.'

Had this Torretta opened some kind of emporium inside the police station? He thought for a minute about going to see him at his desk, then decided that he didn't give a damn. Mimì Augello came in.

'Gimme a cigarette,' said Montalbano.

'I stopped smoking.'

The inspector looked at him, flabbergasted.

'Did your doctor forbid it?'

'No, it was my own decision.'

'I see. Have you switched to cocaine?'

'What's this bullshit you're saying?'

'It's not bullshit, Mimì. Nowadays they're passing very severe laws against smoking, practically persecuting smokers and copying the Americans yet again. But at the same time there's more and more tolerance shown for cocaine addicts. After all, everybody uses the stuff, under-secretaries, politicians, businessmen … The fact is that if you smoke a cigarette, the guy next to you can accuse you of poisoning him with second-hand smoke, whereas there's no such thing as second-hand cocaine. In short, cocaine causes less social damage than smoking. How many lines do you snort a day, Mimì?'

'Got your dander up today, I guess. Letting off steam?'

'A little.'

What the hell was happening? Catarella getting names

right, Mimì turning virtuous... Inside the microcosm that was the Vigàta Police headquarters, something was changing, and this too was a sign that it was time to go.

'I have to go to a meeting at the commissioner's this afternoon. I also asked to speak with the commissioner in private afterwards. I'm giving him my resignation. You're the only one who knows. If the commissioner accepts it, I'll tell everyone this evening.'

'Do whatever you want,' Mimì said rudely, getting up and heading to the door.

Then he stopped and turned around.

'For your information, I stopped smoking because it could hurt Beba and the baby on the way. As for resigning, you're probably right to leave. You've lost your spark, your muscle tone, your irony, your mental agility, and even your meanness.'

'Fuck you, Mimì, and get me Catarella!' the inspector yelled as Mimì left.

Two seconds were all it took for Catarella to materialize.

'Your orders, Chief.'

'See if Torretta has a soft pack of red Multifilters and a lighter.'

Catarella seemed unfazed by the request. He disappeared, then reappeared with the cigarettes and lighter. The inspector gave him the money and went out wondering if the Torretta Emporium had any socks, as he would soon be needing some. Once he hit the street, he felt like having a proper cup of espresso. In the cafe next to the station, the television, as usual, was on. It was twelve thirty, time for the TeleVigàta lunchtime news. Anchor-woman Carla Rosso's talking head appeared, running through the news items in an order of importance based on the audience's preferences. First she reported on a drama of jealousy run amok, with an eighty-year-old man stabbing his seventy-year-old wife to death. Then came the violent crash of a caravan and a car with three passengers, all dead; an armed robbery at a branch of the Credito di Montelusa; an old tub with a hundred or so refugees spotted out at sea; and another case of piracy on the roads, where an immigrant boy, whom the authorities were unable to identify, was struck and killed by a hit-and-run driver.

Montalbano drank his coffee alone and undisturbed, paid, said goodbye, went outside, lit a cigarette, smoked it, stamped it out in the doorway of the station, greeted Catarella, went into his office, and sat down, when all of a sudden the cafe's television appeared on the wall before him, with Carla Rosso's talking head silently opening and closing its mouth as her words echoed inside the inspector's head:

'An immigrant boy, who the authorities were unable to identify ...'

All at once he found himself back on his feet, hurriedly retracing his last steps, almost without knowing why. Or rather, he did know why, but didn't want to admit it: the rational side of his brain was rejecting what his irrational side was telling him to do at that moment – that is, to obey an absurd presentiment.

'Did you forget something?' asked the barman, seeing the inspector rush in.

He didn't even answer. They'd changed the channel. There was some sitcom on, and you could see the 'Free Channel' logo in the corner.

'Turn it back to TeleVigàta, immediately!' the inspector said in a voice so cold and deep that the barman turned pale as he dashed to the set.

He'd arrived in time. The news was considered so unimportant that there weren't even any images accompanying the report. Carla Rosso said that early that morning, a peasant on his way to work in his field had seen an unidentified car knock down a small non-European boy. The man had phoned for help, but the boy was dead on arrival at Montechiaro Hospital. After which Carla Rosso, a smile slicing her face in two, wished everyone a good lunch and disappeared.

A kind of fight broke out inside the inspector's body, pitting his legs, which wanted to leave in a hurry, against his brain, which insisted on a normal, easy gait. Apparently they reached a compromise, and as a result, as he headed back to the station, Montalbano looked like one of those mechanical dolls whose spring is beginning to unwind, making it lurch forward in fits and starts, first fast, then slow, then fast again.

He stopped in the doorway and yelled:

'Mimì! Mimì!'

'Somebody performing *La Bohème* today?' enquired Augello when he appeared.

'Listen closely. I can't go to that meeting at the commissioner's. You go. The papers you need to show him are on my desk.'

'What's wrong with you?'

'Nothing. And give him my apologies. Tell him I'll talk to him another time about that personal matter.'

'What excuse should I give him?'

'One of those excuses you're so good at inventing when you don't come in to work.'

'Want to tell me where you're going?'

'No.'

Concerned, Augello lingered in the doorway and watched him leave.

Provided that the tyres – by now smooth as a baby's bottom – held the road, that the fuel tank didn't spring an irreparable leak, that the motor could bear a speed greater than fifty miles per hour, and that there wouldn't be much traffic, Montalbano figured he could make it to Montechiaro Hospital in an hour and a half.

*

At a certain point, as he was racing along full-throttle, in danger of crashing into a tree or another car – since he'd never in his life been a good driver – he felt utterly ridiculous. On what basis in fact was he doing what he was doing? There must be hundreds of little black boys in Sicily. What made him think the little kid run over by the car was the same one he'd taken by the hand on the wharf a few nights before? Of one thing, however, he was certain: to ease his conscience, he absolutely had to see that boy, otherwise the doubt would keep stewing inside him, tormenting him. If it happened not to be the same boy, so much the better.

It would mean that the family reunion, as Riguccio called it, had been a success.

*

At Montechiaro Hospital, the staff let Montalbano talk to one Dr Quarantino, an affable, courteous young man.

'Inspector, when the boy got here he was already dead. I think he must have died upon impact. Which was very, very violent. So violent it broke his back.'

Montalbano felt something like a cold wind envelop him.

'He was hit in the back, you say?'

'Yes. The boy was probably standing at the side of the road when a car came up at high speed behind him and skidded out of control,' Dr Quarantino hypothesized.

'Do you know who brought him here?'

'Yes. One of our ambulances, which was summoned by the Road Police after they rushed to the scene.'

'The Montechiaro Road Police?'

'Yes.'

He finally made up his mind to ask the question he hadn't had the strength to ask thus far.

'Is the boy still here?'

'Yes, in the morgue.'

'Could I . . . could I see him?'

'Of course. Please follow me.'

They went down a corridor, got in a lift, went underground, walked down another corridor much drearier than the previous one, and at last the doctor stopped in front of a door.

'Here we are.'

A cramped, cold, dimly lit room. A small table, two chairs, a metal shelf. Also metal was one of the walls, though in reality the wall consisted of refrigerated cells that slid out like drawers. Quarantino pulled one out. The little body was covered by a sheet. The doctor began to lift the sheet gently, and Montalbano first saw the wide-open eyes, the very same eyes with which the little boy had begged him to let him run away, to let him escape, when they were on the wharf. There was no doubt about it.

'That's enough,' he said in a voice so soft it sounded like a breath.

He could tell, from the look Quarantino gave him, that his face had drastically changed expression.

'Did you know him?'

'Yes.'

Quarantino closed the drawer.

'Can we go?'

'Yes.'

But the inspector couldn't move. His legs refused to budge; they were like two pieces of wood. Despite the cold inside the little chamber, he felt his shirt all drenched with sweat. Then he forced himself, getting dizzy in the process, and at last began to walk.

✻

At Road Police headquarters they explained to him where the accident had occurred. Two and a half miles outside Montechiaro, along an unauthorized, unpaved road linking an unauthorized seaside village called Spigonella with another seaside village, also unauthorized, called Tricase. The road did not proceed in a straight line, but rather made long detours inland to service other unauthorized houses inhabited by people who preferred the air of the countryside to that of the sea. One officer was so kind as to make an extremely precise drawing of the route the inspector had to take to find the place.

✻

Not only was the road unpaved, but one could clearly tell that it actually was an old goat path whose countless holes had been poorly and only partially filled. How could a car ever have driven down it at high speed without risking a breakdown? Was it being chased by another car? Rounding a bend, Montalbano realized he'd reached the right place. At the base of a mound of gravel to the right of the path was a small bouquet of wildflowers. He stopped the car and got out to have a better look. The mound looked gouged out on one side, as if from a powerful impact. The gravel was stained with large, dark splotches of dried blood. From where he stood, he could see no houses, only cultivated fields. Off to the side, about a hundred yards down the path, a peasant was hoeing. Montalbano walked towards him, having trouble keeping his footing on the soft ground. The peasant was about sixty, thin and bent, and didn't bother to look up.

'Good afternoon.'

'Good afternoon.'

'I'm a police inspector.'

'I figgered.'

How so? Better not to dwell on it.

'Was it you who put the flowers in the gravel?'

'Yessir.'

'Did you know that little boy?'

'Never seen 'im afore.'

'So why did you put those flowers there?'

'He was a creature of God, not no animal.'

'Did you see the accident happen?'

'I both seen it and didn't see it.'

'What do you mean?'

'Come over here and follow me.'

Montalbano followed him. After about ten paces, the peasant stopped.

'At seven o'clock this morning I was here, hoeing this

spot right here. All of a sudden I hear this terrible scream. I look up and see a little kid run out from behind the bend. He's runnin like a rabbit and screamin.'

'Did you understand what he was saying?'

'No sir. When he's over there by that carob, a car come speedin really fast around the bend. The kid turned round to look and then tried to git off the road. Maybe he was tryin a come towards me. But then I din't see 'im no more cause he's hid behind that mound of gravel. Then the car swerved behind 'im, but I din't see no more. I heard a kind of thud. Then the car went into reverse, went back out on the road, an' disappeared around the next bend.'

Though there was no chance the man was mistaken, Montalbano wanted to make especially sure.

'Was that car being followed by another?'

'No sir. It was alone.'

'And would you say it deliberately swerved behind the boy?'

'I dunno if he did it 'liberately, but he swerved all right.'

'Did you manage to see the licence-plate number?'

'You kiddin? Have a look fo' y'self an' see if you c'n see over there.'

Indeed, it was impossible. The difference in elevation between the field and the road was too great.

'What did you do next?'

'I started runnin toward the mound. But when I got there I knew 'mmediately the kid was dead or just about.

So I run back to my house, which you can't see from here, an' I called Montechiaro.'

'Did you tell the Road Police what you just told me?'

'No sir.'

'Why not?'

''Cause they din't ask.'

Iron-clad logic: no question, no answer.

'Well, I'm asking you straight out: do you think they did it on purpose?'

The peasant must have already pondered this question a long time. He answered with a question.

'Coun't the car swerve without wanting to, 'cause it hit a rock?'

'Maybe. But you, deep down, what do *you* think?'

'I don't think, Mr 'Nspecter. I don't wanna think no more. The world's become too evil.'

The last statement was decisive. Obviously the old peasant had a very clear idea of what happened. The kid had been deliberately run over. Butchered for some inexplicable reason. But the peasant had immediately wanted to expunge that idea from his head. The world had become too evil. Better not to think about it.

Montalbano wrote down the phone number of the Vigàta Police on a scrap of paper and handed it to the peasant.

'That's the phone number of my office in Vigàta.'

'What'm I supposed to do with it?'

'Nothing. Just hang on to it. If by chance the boy's mother or father or some other relative comes asking about him, find out where they live and then tell me.'

'As you wish, sir.'

'Good day.'

'Good day.'

✻

The climb back up to the road was harder than the descent. He ran out of breath. At last he reached his car, opened the door, and got in, but instead of starting the motor he just sat there, immobile, arms on the steering wheel, head resting on his arms, eyes shut tight, trying to blot out the world. Just like the peasant, who had resumed hoeing and would continue to do so until night fell. Suddenly a thought came into his head like an ice-cold blade that, after cleaving his brain, descended and stopped in the middle of his chest, running him all the way through: the valiant, brilliant Inspector Salvo Montalbano had taken that boy by his little hand and, ever willing to help, turned him over to his executioners.

EIGHT

It was too early to hole up in Marinella, but he decided to go home anyway, without first stopping at the office. The genuine rage that was churning inside him made his blood boil and had surely given him a slight fever. He was better off trying to get the anger out of his system alone and not taking it out on his men at the station, grasping at the slightest excuse. His first victim was a vase someone had given him, which he had hated right from the start. Raising it high over his head with both hands, he dashed it to the floor with great satisfaction, accompanied by a vigorous curse. After the loud thud, however, Montalbano was flabbergasted to find that the vase hadn't suffered so much as a scratch.

How could that be? He bent down, grabbed it, raised it again, and hurled it down with all his might. Nothing. And that wasn't all: now a floor tile was cracked. Was he going to wreck his house just to destroy that damned vase? He went out to his car, opened the glove compartment, took out his pistol, went back inside, grabbed the vase, went out on the veranda, onto the beach, walked down to the water's edge, laid the vase down on the sand, took ten steps back, cocked the pistol, aimed, fired, and missed.

'Murderer!'

It was a woman's voice. He turned around to look. From the balcony of a house in the distance, two figures were waving their arms at him.

'Murderer!'

That time it was a man's voice. Who the hell were they? Then he remembered: Mr and Mrs Bausan from Treviso! The couple that had made him make an arse of himself by appearing naked on television. Telling them in his mind to fuck off, he took careful aim and fired. This time the vase exploded. Satisfied, he headed back home accompanied by an increasingly distant chorus of 'Murderer! Murderer!'

He got undressed, stepped into the shower, and even shaved and put on fresh clothes as if he was going out to see people. Whereas he was only going to see himself, but he wanted to look good. He went out and sat on the veranda to think. Even if he'd not expressed it in words or in his mind, he had definitely made a promise to that pair of gaping eyes staring out at him from their refrigerated drawer. And he was reminded of a novel by Dürrenmatt, in which a police inspector's whole life is consumed trying to find a young girl's killer, to keep the promise he'd made to her parents ... But the killer has died in the meantime, and the inspector doesn't know this. He's chasing a ghost. In the case of the little black boy, however, the victim was also a ghost; he didn't know his name, nationality, nothing. Just as he knew nothing about the victim in the other case he was working on, the unknown forty-year-old who'd been drowned. Most importantly, these weren't even proper investigations; no case files had been opened. The unknown man was, in bureaucratic terms, dead by drowning; the little kid was one of the countless victims of hit-and-run drivers. What, officially speaking, was there to investigate? Less than nothing. *Nada de nada.*

Now this is the kind of investigation that might interest me after I retire, the inspector reflected. *If I work on it now, does it mean I feel as though I'm already retired?*

A great wave of melancholy swept over him. The inspector had two proven methods for combating melancholy: the first was to bury himself in bed, covers pulled up over his head; the second was to stuff himself with food. He glanced at his watch. Too early to go to bed; if he fell asleep now he was liable to wake up at three in the morning, and then he would really go nuts fidgeting about the house. That left only the food. Besides, he remembered that at midday he hadn't had time to eat. He went into the kitchen and opened the refrigerator. For whatever reason, Adelina had prepared him beef roulades. Not what he needed. He went out, got in the car, and went to the Trattoria Da Enzo. During the first course, spaghetti in squid ink, the melancholy started to recede. By the time he'd finished the second — crispy fried calamaretti — his melancholy, put to rout, disappeared behind the horizon. Back home in Marinella, the gears in his brain felt smooth and oiled, like new again. He went back out on the veranda and sat down.

✻

First off, he had to give credit to Livia for having got it right — that is, for having understood that the boy's behaviour on the wharf had been very strange indeed. Obviously the kid was trying to take advantage of the momentary confusion so he could escape. And he hadn't succeeded because he, the brilliant, sublime Inspector Montalbano, had prevented him. But, even assuming this whole business involved a troubled family reunion, to use Riguccio's expression, why would anyone so brutally murder a little boy like that? Because he had the bad habit of running away no matter where he happened to be? But how many kids were there the world over, of all colours — white, black, yellow — whose greatest fantasy is to run away from home? Hundreds of thousands, surely. And are they punished by death? Surely not. And so? Maybe he was slaughtered because he was restless, talked back, didn't obey daddy, or refused to eat his soup? Come on! In the light of that killing, Riguccio's hypothesis became ridiculous. There had to be something else. That kid must have been carrying something big on his shoulders, from the outset, whatever his country of origin.

The best thing was to start over from the beginning, neglecting none of the details that at first glance might have seemed entirely useless. And to proceed in stages, without piling up too much information all at once. That evening, he'd been sitting in his office, waiting till it was time to go to Ciccio Albanese's house so the captain could tell him about sea currents and also, certainly not secondarily, to gorge himself on Signora Albanese's striped surmullet. At a certain point, Deputy Commissioner Riguccio calls the station: he's at the port, processing a hundred and fifty illegal immigrants; he's broken his glasses, and asks if anybody's got a pair that might work for him. Montalbano finds a pair and decides to bring them to Riguccio himself. When he arrives at the wharf, one of the patrol boats has lowered its gangway. The first person to come out is a fat, pregnant woman who is taken directly to an ambulance. Then four men come down, and when they're almost at the bottom of the gangway, they stumble briefly over a little boy who seems to have slipped between their legs. The boy manages to evade the policemen at the scene and starts running towards the old silo. The inspector runs after him and senses the kid's presence in an alley full of refuse. The kid realizes there's no way out and surrenders, literally. The inspector takes him by the hand and is bringing him back to the area near the gangplank when he notices a woman, rather young, wailing in despair as two other small children hang from her skirts. As soon as she sees him with the boy, the woman runs towards them. Apparently she's

policeman would have called over the doctor who, as always, was there with them. Why wasn't the doctor consulted? He wasn't consulted because there wasn't time. The ambulance's sudden arrival and the paramedic's diagnosis had steered events in the direction desired by the director. Yes, director. That whole scene had been prearranged and staged with great intelligence.

Despite the hour, he grabbed the phone.

'Fazio? Montalbano here.'

'There's no news, Chief, otherwise I'd have—'

'Save your breath. I want to ask you something. Were you planning to continue your search tomorrow?'

'Yes.'

'I want you to take care of something for me first.'

'Yessir.'

'At San Gregorio Hospital, there's an ambulance worker with a moustache, a very thin man of about fifty. I want to know everything about him, the known and the unknown. Get my drift?'

'Yessir, absolutely.'

He hung up and called the San Gregorio.

'Is nurse Agata Militello there?'

'Just a minute. Yes, she's here.'

'I'd like to speak to her.'

'She's on duty. We have orders not—'

'Listen, this is Inspector Montalbano. It's a serious matter.'

'Please wait while I look for her.'

When he was beginning to lose hope, he heard the nurse's voice.

'Is that you, Inspector?'

'Yes. I'm sorry if I—'

'Not at all. What can I do for you?'

'I need to see you and talk to you. As soon as possible.'

'Listen, Inspector, I'm on the night shift and would like to sleep in a bit tomorrow morning. Could we meet around eleven?'

'Certainly. Where?'

'We could meet in front of the hospital.'

He was about to say yes, but thought better of it. What if the ambulance worker were to see them together?

'I'd rather we met in front of your house.'

'All right. I'm at Via della Regione, number 28. See you tomorrow.'

*

He slept like an innocent cherub with no problems or thoughts, as he always did when he started an investigation on what seemed to be the right foot. The next morning he arrived at the office fresh and smiling. On his desk was a hand-delivered envelope addressed to him. There was no indication of the sender.

'Catarella!'

'Your orders, Chief!'

'Who brought this letter?'

'Pontius Pilate, Chief. Brought it here last night.'

He put it in his pocket. He would read it later. Or maybe never. Mimì Augello came in a few minutes later.

'How'd it go with the commissioner?' Montalbano asked.

'He seemed down, less self-assured than usual. Obviously all he brought back from Rome was a lot of hot air. He said it's clear now that the flow of illegal immigrants has shifted from the Adriatic to the Mediterranean and that it'll be harder than ever to stop. Apparently the people at the top are a little slow to acknowledge this fact. But then again, they're also slow to acknowledge that petty theft is up, not to mention armed robbery... They just sing in chorus "*Tutto va ben, mia nobile marchesa*", while we're supposed to keep plodding along with the little we have.'

'Did you apologize for my absence?'

'Yes.'

'And what'd he say?'

'What did you want him to do, Salvo? Start crying? He merely said: fine. Full stop. Now tell me what was the matter with you yesterday.'

'I had a problem.'

'Salvo, who do you think you're fooling? First you tell me you want to see the commissioner to tender your resignation, then fifteen minutes later you change your mind and tell me I have to go to the commissioner's instead. What kind of problem?'

'If you really want to know...'

He told him the whole story of the little boy. When he'd finished, Mimì was silent and pensive.

'Something not add up for you?' Montalbano asked.

'No, it all adds up, but only up to a point.'

'And what would that be?'

'You directly connect the boy's murder with his attempt to run away on the wharf. I'm not so sure about that.'

'Come on, Mimì! Why else would he have done it, then?'

'Let me tell you something. Last month a friend of mine went to New York and stayed with an American friend of his. One day they went out to eat. My friend ordered an enormous steak with potatoes on the side. He couldn't eat it all and left some of it on his plate. After clearing the table, the waiter came back with a little bag containing what my friend hadn't eaten. My friend takes the bag and, outside the restaurant, sees a group of bums and starts walking towards them to give them the bag with his leftovers. But his American friend stops him, telling him the bums won't accept it. If he feels like being charitable, he should give them fifty cents, he says. "Why won't they accept the bag with half a steak in it?" my friend asks. "Because there are people here who give them poisoned food, the way they do with stray dogs," he says. See my point?'

'No.'

'It's possible that the little boy, caught by surprise at the side of the road, was deliberately run over just for fun, or in a fit of racism, by some goddamned son of a bitch, some nameless bastard who had nothing to do with the kid's arrival here.'

Montalbano let out a deep sigh.

'I wish! If that were really what happened, I would feel less guilty. Unfortunately, I'm pretty convinced the whole affair has a precise logic of its own.'

*

Agata Militello was a well-groomed woman of about forty, good-looking but tending dangerously towards plumpness. She was a garrulous sort and in fact did almost all the talking during the hour she spent with the inspector. She said she was in a bad mood that morning because her son, an undergraduate ('You know, Inspector, I had the bad luck to fall in love at age seventeen with a rascal who left me as soon as he learned I was expecting'), wanted to get married ('But I say, can't you wait? What's the hurry? Meanwhile you can do whatever you want, and then we'll see'). She also said that the hospital management were cynical bastards who took advantage of her, knowing she would come running every time they asked her to work overtime because she had a heart of gold.

'It happened here,' she said suddenly, coming to a halt.

They were on a short street with no residences or shops, practically only the backs of two large buildings.

'But there's not a single house here,' said Montalbano.

'You're right. We're behind the hospital, which is this

building here on the right. I always take this route, because that way I can enter through A&E, which is the first door on the right once you turn this corner.'

'So the woman with the three children must have left A&E, turned left, taken this street, and then was greeted by that car.'

'Exactly.'

'Did you notice whether the car was coming from the direction of the emergency ward or from the opposite direction?'

'No, I couldn't tell.'

'When the car stopped, could you see how many people were inside?'

'Before the woman and her children got in?'

'Yes.'

'There was only the driver.'

'Did you notice anything in particular about the man driving?'

'How could I, Inspector? He stayed in the car the whole time! But he wasn't black, if that's what you mean.'

'He wasn't? He was one of us?'

'Yes, but can you tell the difference between a Sicilian and a Tunisian? You know, one time, I—'

'How many ambulances does the hospital have?' the inspector interrupted.

'Four, but they're not enough. And there's no money to buy even one more.'

'How many men are there in an ambulance when it's on duty?'

'Two. We have a shortage of personnel. One paramedic and a driver, who helps out.'

'Do you know them all?'

'Of course.'

He wanted to ask her about the gaunt paramedic with the moustache but didn't. The woman talked too much. She was liable to run to the man afterwards and tell him the inspector had asked about him.

'Shall we go and have a coffee?'

'Yes, thank you, Inspector. Even though I'm not supposed to. You know, one time I had four coffees in a row, and . . .'

*

Fazio was waiting for him at headquarters, impatient to resume his search for information on the dead man he'd found in the sea. Fazio was like a dog that, once he picked up a scent, didn't relent until he'd flushed out his quarry.

'Chief, the ambulance worker's name is Gaetano Marzilla.'

He stopped.

'Yeah? Is that all?' asked Montalbano, surprised.

'Chief, can we make a deal?'

'A deal?'

'Let me indulge a little in my records office complex, as

you call it, and afterwards I'll tell you what I found out about him.'

'It's a deal,' the inspector said, resigned.

Fazio's eyes sparkled with contentment. He pulled a small piece of paper out of his pocket and began reading.

'Gaetano Marzilla, born in Montelusa on 6 October 1960, son of the late Stefano Marzilla and Antonia née Diblasi, resident of Montelusa, Via Francesco Crispi 18. Married Elisabetta Cappuccino, born at Ribera on 14 February, 1963, daughter of Emanuele Cappuccino and Eugenia née Ricottilli, who—'

'Stop right there or I'll shoot,' said Montalbano.

'OK, OK. I'm satisfied,' said Fazio, putting the piece of paper back in his pocket.

'So, do we want to talk about serious matters now?'

'Sure. This Marzilla's been working at the hospital ever since getting his nursing degree. His wife came with a modest gift shop in her dowry, but the shop burned down three years ago.'

'Arson?'

'Yes, but the place wasn't insured. Rumour has it that it was burned down because Marzilla got tired of paying the protection money. And you know what Marzilla did?'

'Fazio, those kinds of questions only piss me off. I don't know a damned thing! You're the one who's supposed to be filling me in!'

'Marzilla learned his lesson and started coughing up the protection money. Feeling safe, he bought a warehouse adjacent to the shop and expanded and renovated every-thing. To make a long story short, he got covered in debt, and since business is bad, the loan sharks have him by the throat now, according to the gossip. Lately the poor guy's so desperate he's looking left and right for any spare change he can get his hands on.'

'I absolutely must speak with this man,' said Montal-bano, after remaining silent a few moments. 'And as soon as possible.'

'What are we going to do? We certainly can't arrest the guy,' said Fazio.

'No. Who ever said anything about arresting him? On the other hand ...'

'On the other hand?'

'If he got wind ...'

'Of what?'

'Nothing, I just thought of something. You know the address of his shop?'

'Of course, Chief. Via Palermo 34.'

'Thanks. Now go and pound the pavement some more.'

NINE

After Fazio left, he sat and pondered his course of action until he had it all clear in his mind. He called in Galluzzo.

'Listen, I want you to go to the Bulone printworks and have them make a bunch of business cards for you.'

'With my name?' asked Galluzzo, perplexed.

'Come on, Gallù, are you acting like Catarella now? With my name.'

'And what should I tell them to write?'

'The essentials. Salvo Montalbano and, underneath, Chief Inspector, Vigàta Police. On the bottom left, have them put our telephone number. Ten or so will be enough.'

'While we're at it, Chief—'

'You want me to order a thousand? So I can wallpaper my bathroom with 'em? Ten'll be more than enough. And I want them on my desk by four o'clock this afternoon. No excuses. Now hurry, before they close for lunch.'

It was time to eat. Since most people were at home, he might as well try. He picked up the phone.

'Hallo? Who tokin?' said the voice of a woman who must have come from at least as far away as Burkina Faso.

'This is Inspector Montalbano. Is Signora Ingrid there?'

'You wait.'

By now it was tradition. Whenever he called up Ingrid, a housekeeper from a country nowhere to be found on the map always answered.

'Hi, Salvo? What's up?'

'I'm going to need a little help from you. Are you free this afternoon?'

'Yes. I have an engagement around six.'

'That should be more than enough time. Can we meet in Montelusa, in front of the Vittoria Café at four-thirty?'

'Sure. See you later.'

*

At home he found a casserole of tender, mischievous *pasta 'ncasciata* (he suffered from improper use of adjectives and couldn't define it any better than this) in the oven and feasted on it. Then he changed, putting on a grey double-breasted suit, a pale blue shirt, and a red tie. He wanted to look like a cross between white-collar and shady. Afterwards, he sat out on the veranda and sipped a coffee while smoking a cigarette.

Before going out, he looked for a greenish, vaguely Tyrolean-style hat he hardly ever wore and a pair of glasses with plain lenses that he'd used once but couldn't remember why. At four o'clock he returned to the office and found a small box with business cards on his desk. He took three and put them in his wallet. He went back outside, opened the boot of his car, where he kept a Humphrey Bogart-style trench coat, put this on, along with the hat and glasses, and drove off.

*

Seeing him appear before her in that get-up, Ingrid began laughing so hard that tears started running down her cheeks and she had to dash into the cafe and lock herself in the bathroom.

When she came out, however, the giggles got the better of her again. Montalbano was stone-faced.

'Get in the car, I've no time to waste.'

Ingrid obeyed, making a tremendous effort to refrain from laughing.

'Do you know that gift shop at number 34, Via Palermo?'

'No, why?'

'Because that's where we're going.'

'What for?'

'To select a present for a girlfriend of yours who's getting married. And I want you to call me Emilio.'

Ingrid literally exploded. Her laughter burst out uncontrollably. She put her head in her hands, and he couldn't tell if she was laughing or crying.

'OK, I'm taking you home,' the inspector said in a huff.

'No, wait a minute, come on.'

She blew her nose twice, wiped away her tears.

'Tell me what I'm supposed to do, Emilio.'

Montalbano explained.

The shop's sign said *Cappuccino*, in big letters, and below, in smaller characters, *Silverware, Gifts, Bridal Registries*. The undoubtedly fancy display windows featured an array of glittering objects of questionable taste. Montalbano tried to open the door, but it was locked. Fear of robberies, apparently. He pushed a button, and somebody opened the door from within. Inside there was only a fortyish woman, petite and well dressed, but clearly nervous and on the defensive.

'Good afternoon,' she said, but without the welcoming smile usually reserved for clients. 'What can I do for you?'

Montalbano was certain she was not an employee but Signora Cappuccino in person.

'Good afternoon,' Ingrid replied. 'A friend of ours is getting married, and Emilio and I would like to give her a silver platter as a present. Could I see what you have?'

'Certainly,' said Signora Cappuccino, and she began taking silver platters off the shelves, each one more vulgar than the last, and setting them down on the counter. Montalbano, meanwhile, was looking around 'in a clearly suspicious manner', as the newspapers and police reports like to say. Finally Ingrid called him over.

'Come, Emilio.'

Montalbano approached and Ingrid showed him two platters.

'I can't decide between these two. Which do you prefer?'

While pretending to waver, the inspector noticed that Signora Cappuccino was stealing glances at him whenever she could. Maybe she'd recognized him, as he was hoping.

'Come on, Emilio, make up your mind,' Ingrid egged him on.

At last Montalbano made up his mind. As Signora Cappuccino was wrapping the platter, Ingrid had a brilliant idea of her own.

'Emilio, look, what a beautiful bowl! Wouldn't that look good in our dining room?'

Montalbano shot a withering glance at her and muttered something incomprehensible.

'Come on, Emilio, please let's buy it. I just love it!' Ingrid insisted, her eyes sparkling with amusement from the joke she was playing on him.

'Do you want it?' Signora Cappuccino asked him.

'Another time,' the inspector said firmly.

Signora Cappuccino then moved over to the cash register and rang up the purchase. When Montalbano reached into the back pocket of his trousers to extract his wallet, it got stuck and all its contents fell to the floor. The inspector bent down to pick up the various notes, cards, and slips of paper.

Then he stood up and with his right foot slid a calling card he'd purposely left on the floor closer to the table supporting the cash register. The sham had been a perfect success. They left.

'You were so mean, Emilio, not to buy me that bowl!' Ingrid said, pretending to be upset when they got in the car. Then, changing her tone: 'Was I good?'

'You were great.'

'What are we going to do with the platter?'

'You can keep it.'

'I'm not going to let you off so easily. Tonight we're eating out. I'm taking you to a place where the fish is out of this world.'

Not a good idea. Montalbano was certain their play-acting would yield immediate results, and he preferred to wait in his office.

'How about tomorrow night?'

'All right.'

*

'Ahh, Chief, Chief!' shrieked Catarella the moment Montalbano entered the office.

'What is it?'

'I been true the whole archive, Chief. I can't see no more, I got spots in front o' my eyeses. There in't nobody otherwise that looks like the dead swimmer looks. Only Errera. Chief, in't it possible it's possibly Errera hisself?'

'Cat, the people in Cosenza told us Errera's dead and buried!'

'OK, Chief, but in't it possible 'e came back to life and then went back to death in the water?'

'Are you trying to give me a headache, Cat?'

'Perish the tot, Chief! What'm I sposta do wit' dese photos?'

'Leave 'em here on the desk. We'll give 'em to Fazio later.'

✻

After two hours of fruitless waiting, an irresistible wave of somnolence came over him. He cleared a space amidst the papers, crossed his arms on the desk, laid his head down on them, and in the twinkling of an eye he was asleep. So deeply, in fact, that when the telephone rang and he reopened his eyes, for a few seconds he didn't know where he was.

'H'lo, Chief. There's somebody wants to talk to you poissonally in poisson.'

'Who is it?'

'That's just it, Chief. He says he don't wanna say what 'is name is.'

'Put 'im on ... Montalbano here. Who is this?'

'Inspector, you came to my wife's shop with a lady this afternoon.'

'I did?'

'Yes, sir, you did.'

'Excuse me, but would you please tell me what your name is?'

'No.'

'Well, then, goodbye.'

He hung up. It was a dangerous move. It was possible that Marzilla had used up what courage he had and wouldn't have the guts to call again. But apparently Marzilla had such a firm bite on the inspector's bait that he needed to call back immediately.

'Inspector, excuse me for that call a minute ago. But try to understand my position. You came into my wife's shop, and she recognized you immediately, even though you were in disguise and went by the name of Emilio. On top of that, my wife found one of your business cards, which had fallen on the floor. You must admit, it's enough to make a guy nervous!'

'Why?'

'Because it's obvious you're investigating something to do with me.'

'If that's what you're worried about, you can relax. The preliminary investigation is over.'

'And I can relax, you say?'

'Absolutely. Until tomorrow, at least.'

He could hear Marzilla's breath stop short.

'What ... what do you mean?'

'I mean that tomorrow I move on to the next phase. The operative phase.'

'And ... what's that mean?'

'You know how these things work, don't you? Arrests, subpoenas, interrogations, prosecutors, reporters ...'

'But I have nothing to do with any of it!'

'With any of what?'

'But ... but ... but ... I dunno, whatever you're investigating ... But then why did you come to the shop?'

'Oh, that? To buy a wedding present.'

'But why were you calling yourself Emilio?'

'The lady I was with likes to call me that. Listen, Marzilla, it's late. I want to go home. See you tomorrow.'

He hung up. Was it possible to be any meaner? He would have bet his balls that within the hour Marzilla would come knocking on his door. He could easily find the address by looking him up in the phone book. As he'd suspected, the ambulance man was up to his neck in what happened on the wharf. Somebody must have ordered him to find a way to get the woman and her three kids into the ambulance and then drop them off outside the hospital's emergency ward. And he'd obeyed.

He got in the car and drove off with all the windows open. He needed to feel some cool, nocturnal sea air on his face.

*

An hour later, as he had lucidly foreseen, a car pulled up in front of his house. A car door slammed, then the doorbell rang. Opening the door, he was greeted by a different Marzilla from the one he'd seen in the hospital car park. Unshaven and haggard, he had a sickly air about him.

'I'm sorry if I—'

'I was expecting you. Come in.'

Montalbano had decided to change tactics, and Marzilla seemed confused by his politeness. He walked in, unsure, then didn't so much sit down as collapse into the chair the inspector offered him.

'I'll do the talking,' said Montalbano. 'We'll waste less time that way.'

The man made a vague gesture of resignation.

'The other evening, at the port, you knew in advance that an immigrant woman with three children would get off the boat and pretend to fall and hurt her leg. Your assignment was to wait there, have the ambulance ready, and not get tied up by some other job – and then to run up, diagnose a broken leg before the doctor could get there, put the woman and her three kids in the ambulance, and head back to Montelusa. Am I right? Answer only yes or no.'

Marzilla managed to answer only after he'd swallowed and run his tongue over his lips.

'Yes.'

'Good. When you got to San Gregorio Hospital, you were supposed to drop the woman and her kids off in front of A&E, without accompanying them inside. You were even lucky enough to get an urgent call to go to Scroglitti, which gave you a good excuse for acting the way you did. Answer.'

'Yes.'

'Was the ambulance driver your accomplice?'

'Yes. I slip him a hundred euro each time.'

'How many times have you done this?'

'Twice.'

'And were there children with the adults both times?'

Marzilla swallowed two or three times before answering.
'Yes.'

'Where do you sit during these runs?'

'It depends. Sometimes in front with the driver, sometimes in the back, with the people we're carrying.'

'And during the run I'm investigating, where did you
sit?'

'For a while, in front.'

'Then you went in the back?'

Marzilla was sweating. He was in trouble.

'Yes.'

'Why?'

'Could I have some water?'

'No.'

Marzilla gave him a frightened look.

'If you won't tell me yourself, I'll tell you. You had to
go in the back because one of the kids, the oldest, the six-
year-old, wanted at all costs to get out of the car, he wanted
to escape. Am I right?'

Marzilla nodded yes.

'What did you do then?'

The medic said something so softly that the inspector
didn't so much hear it as intuit it.

'Gave him a shot? To put him to sleep?'

'No. A sedative.'

'Who held the kid down?'

'His mother. Or whoever she was.'

'And what were the other kids doing?'

'Crying.'

'Was the kid you gave the shot to also crying?'

'No.'

'What was he doing?'

'He was biting his lips. Till they bled.'

Montalbano stood up slowly. He felt a kind of tingling in his legs.

'Please look at me.'

The medic raised his head and looked at him. The first slap, to the left cheek, was so fierce that it turned the man's head almost completely around; the second caught him just as he was turning back around and cuffed his nose, triggering a stream of blood. The man didn't even try to wipe it off, letting the blood stain his shirt and jacket. Montalbano sat back down.

'You're getting my floor all dirty. The bathroom's down the hall on the right. Go and clean yourself up. The kitchen's across the hall. There should be some ice in the freezer. You know what to do, being a nurse when you're not torturing small children.'

The whole time the man was fussing about in the bathroom and kitchen, Montalbano tried hard not to think about the scene Marzilla had just described to him, that hell shrunken down to the little space inside the ambulance, the terror in those eyes open wide on the violence . . .

And it was he who had taken that child by the hand

and turned him over to the horror. He couldn't forgive himself... It was no use repeating to himself that he'd thought he was doing the right thing... He mustn't think about it, mustn't give into the rage, if he wanted to continue the interrogation. Marzilla returned. He'd made an ice pack with his handkerchief and held this over his nose with one hand, his head bent slightly backwards. He sat down in front of the inspector without a word.

'Now I'll tell you why you got so scared when I came to your shop. You had just learned that your bosses had to kill that boy, the one you'd given the shot of sedatives to. Had to cut him down like some wild animal. Am I right?'

'Yes.'

'And so you got scared. Because you're a two-bit hood, a sleazeball, a piece of shit, but you don't have the stuff to be an accomplice to murder. You can tell me later how you found out that the kid you were involved with was the same one they ran over with their car. Now it's your turn to talk. But I'll save you a little breath by telling you that I already know that you're swimming in debt and need money, a lot of money, to pay off the loan sharks. Now go on.'

Marzilla began to talk. The two hard slaps the inspector had dealt him must have dazed him, but they also seemed to have calmed him down a bit. By this point, what was done was done.

'When the banks refused to give me any more loans, I risked losing everything I had. So I started asking the people I knew where I might get a helping hand. They gave me a name and I went to talk to the person. That's how it started. It's worse than being broke; I'm ruined. The guy lent me the money, but at an interest rate so high I'm ashamed to tell you. I scraped by for a while, then I couldn't take it any longer. Then, about two months ago, this man made me an offer.'

'Tell me his name.'

Marzilla shook his head, which he kept tilted backwards.

'I'm scared, Inspector. He's liable to have me and my wife killed.'

'OK, go on. What was this offer he made you?'

'He said he needed to help some immigrant families get back together here. Apparently their husbands had found work here, but since they were illegals, they couldn't bring their wives and children over. In exchange for my help, he would reduce some of the interest I owed him.'

'A fixed percentage?'

'No, Inspector. We were supposed to discuss it each time.'

'How did he let you know when it was time to act?'

'He would phone me the day before a scheduled arrival. He would describe the people and what they were supposed to do to get taken aboard the ambulance. The first time it all went smoothly. There was an old woman with two little kids. But the second time it went the way I said, and the oldest kid rebelled.'

Marzilla stopped and heaved a deep sigh.

'You've got to believe me, Inspector. I couldn't sleep. I kept seeing the scene before my eyes, the woman holding him down, me with the syringe, the other kids crying, and I couldn't fall asleep. A couple of days ago, at about ten in the morning, I went to see the man about reducing my interest. But he said this time he wasn't reducing anything, because the deal had gone sour, the goods were damaged. That's exactly how he put it. But before he sent me away, he said I could still make up for it, since there were some new arrivals coming. I went home feeling depressed. Then I heard on TV that a little immigrant kid had been killed by a hit-and-run driver. And I thought maybe that was what the man meant when he said the goods were damaged. Then you came to my wife's shop, after you'd already been asking questions at the hospital, and ... well, I realized I had to get out, whatever the price.'

Montalbano got up and went out on the veranda. The sea was barely audible, like a small child breathing. He stood there a moment, then went back inside and sat down.

'Listen. So you don't want to give me the name of this ... this gentleman, for lack of a better term.'

'It's not that I don't want to, I can't!' the paramedic nearly screamed.

'OK, calm down. Don't get upset or your nose'll start bleeding again. I'll make you a deal.'

'What kind of deal?'

'You realize I can have you put in jail?'

'Yes.'

'You'd be ruined. You'd lose your job at the hospital, and your wife would have to sell the shop.'

'I understand that.'

'So, if you've got any brains left in your head, you only have to do one thing. Let me know the minute the guy calls you. That's all. We'll take care of everything else.'

'Will you keep me out of it?'

'I can't guarantee you that. But I can try to limit the damage. I give you my word. Now get the hell out of here.'

'Thank you,' said Marzilla, standing up and heading for the door on shaky legs.

'Don't mention it,' Montalbano replied.

*

He didn't go to bed right away. He took out half a bottle of whisky and went out on the veranda to drink it. Before each swig, he raised the bottle in the air. A toast to the little warrior who had fought as long as he could, but didn't make it.

TEN

Horrid, windy morning, wan sun smothered by fast-moving dirt-grey clouds. It was more than enough to top off the inspector's already dark mood. He went in the kitchen, made coffee, drank a first demi-tasse, smoked a cigarette, did what he had to do, got in the shower, shaved, and put on the same clothes he'd been wearing for two days. Before going out, he went back in the kitchen with the intention of drinking another coffee but only managed to fill the demi-tasse halfway, because he spilled the other half on his trousers. Without warning, his hand, entirely on its own, had swerved. Cursing as if to a platoon of Turks lined up before him, he undressed, leaving his suit on a chair so that Adelina could clean and iron it. He emptied the pockets of their contents so he could move them all into the suit he was going to put on. To his surprise he found an unopened envelope in the pile. Where did that come from? Then he remembered. It was the letter Catarella had given him, which he said had been personally delivered by Pontius

Pilate, the journalist. His first impulse was to toss it into the waste-paper basket, but then, for whatever reason, he decided to read it, since he could always choose not to answer. His eyes ran down to the signature at the bottom: Fonso Spàlato, which could easily translate to Pontius Pilate in Catarellese. The letter was rather brief, already a point in favour of the person who'd written it.

> Dear Inspector Montalbano,
>
> I am a freelance journalist. I've written for a variety of newspapers and magazines, but belong to no single one. I have done rather extensive investigations into the Mafia of the Brenta region and arms smuggling from the former Eastern-bloc countries, and for some time now have been devoting much of my time to illegal immigration in the Adriatic and Mediterranean.
>
> A few evenings ago I caught a glimpse of you on the landing wharf at the port, during a typical arrival of refugees. I know you by reputation and thought we might find it mutually useful to meet and exchange ideas (though not for an interview, heaven forbid: I know how much you hate them).
>
> Please find my mobile-phone number at the bottom of the page. I'll be staying on the island another two days.
>
> Sincerely,
>
> Fonso Spàlato

The inspector liked the lean style. He decided to call up the journalist as soon as he got to work, assuming, of course, that the man was still around.

*

The first thing he did when he walked into the station was to call Catarella and Mimì into his office.

'Catarella, listen to me very carefully. A certain Mr Marzilla is supposed to call me. As soon as he does—'

''Scuse me, Chief,' Catarella interrupted, 'what'd you say this Marzilla's name was? Cardilla?'

Montalbano felt reassured. If Catarella was back to screwing up people's names, it meant the end of the world was not yet nigh.

'For the love of the Blessed Virgin, why would he be called Cardilla when you yourself just called him Marzilla?!'

'Did I?' asked an astonished Catarella. 'Then what's the man's name, for Chrissakes?'

The inspector took out a sheet of paper, grabbed a red marker pen, wrote MARZILLA in large block letters on it, and handed it to Catarella.

'Read it.'

Catarella read it correctly.

'Excellent,' said Montalbano. 'I want you to hang that piece of paper next to the switchboard. The minute he calls, you're to put him on the line to me, whether I happen to be here or in Afghanistan. Understand?'

'Yessir, Chief. You go right on ahead to Afghanistan, and I'll put him on for you.'

'Salvo, why did you have me witness this little vaude-ville act?' Augello asked as soon as Catarella left the room.

'Because I want you to ask Catarella, three times in the

morning and three times in the afternoon, if Marzilla has called.'

'Mind telling me who this Marzilla is?'

'I'll tell you if you've been a good boy and done your homework.'

Nothing whatsoever happened for the rest of the morning. Or rather, only routine stuff: a call for the police to intervene in a violent family quarrel that turned into an aggressive face-off between the suddenly reunited family on the one hand, and Gallo and Galluzzo, guilty of trying to make peace, on the other; a report filed by the deputy mayor, who came in pale as a corpse, saying he'd found a rabbit with its throat slashed, nailed to his front door; a drive-by shooting at a man standing at a petrol station who, unharmed, rushed back into his car and drove off into the void before the pump attendant had time to get his licence-plate number; the nearly daily hold-up at a supermarket. Meanwhile, the journalist Spàlato's mobile phone remained stubbornly turned off. In short, if Montalbano wasn't entirely fed up, he was close. He rewarded himself with lunch at the Trattoria Da Enzo.

*

Around four o'clock that afternoon, Fazio phoned in. He was calling on his mobile phone from Spigonella.

'Chief? I've got some news.'

'Let's have it.'

'At least two people here think they saw the dead guy

you found. They recognized him from the photo with the moustache.'

'Do they know what his name was?'

'No.'

'Did he live there?'

'They don't know.'

'Do they know what he was doing around there?'

'No.'

'Well, what the hell do they know?'

Fazio chose not to answer directly.

'Chief, why don't you come out here? That way you can assess the situation yourself. You can either take the coastal road, which is always clogged, or you can come by way of Montechiaro, taking the—'

'I know that road.'

It was the same road he'd taken when he went to see the place where the little kid had been killed. He phoned Ingrid, with whom he was supposed to go out to dinner. She immediately apologized and said she couldn't see him because her husband had invited some friends to dinner without telling her, and she therefore had to play housewife. They arranged that she would come by the station around eight thirty the following evening. If he wasn't there, she would wait.

He tried the journalist's number again, and this time Fonso Spàlato answered.

'Inspector! I was worried you wouldn't call back.'

'Listen, can we meet?'

'When?'

'Immediately, if you want.'

'That'd be hard for me. I had to fly up to Trieste and have spent the whole day either in airports or in planes running late. Fortunately Mama isn't as sick as my sister had me believe.'

'I'm happy to hear it. So?'

'Let's do this. If all goes well, I hope to catch a plane to Rome tomorrow and go on from there. I'll keep you posted.'

✳

At a certain point past Montechiaro, after turning onto the road for Spigonella, the inspector saw the turn for Tricase. At first he hesitated, then made up his mind. He would only lose about ten minutes, at most. He rounded the bend. The peasant was not out working his fields. There was silence, not even a barking dog. The wildflowers at the base of the mound of gravel had wilted.

He had to summon all of his modest driving skills to back the car up that earthquake-riven former goat path and return to the road for Spigonella. Fazio was waiting for him next to his car, which was parked in front of a white-and-red two-storey villa that looked uninhabited. A rough sea roared below.

'Spigonella starts at this house,' said Fazio. 'It's probably better if we take my car.'

Montalbano got in. Fazio turned on the ignition and began to act as his guide.

'Spigonella sits on a rocky plateau. To reach the sea, you have to go up and down stairs that are cut straight into the rock. It must be murder in summertime. You can also reach the sea by car, by taking the road you just took towards Tricase and then coming up this way from there. Got that?'

'Yes.'

'Tricase, on the other hand, is right on the sea, but it's been settled differently.'

'What do you mean?'

'I mean that here in Spigonella these villas were built by people with money – lawyers, doctors, businessmen – whereas in Tricase there're only little houses, one after another, lived in by little people.'

'But the little houses are just as unauthorized as the villas, aren't they?'

'Sure, Chief, but I just meant that here every villa is secluded. See over there? High walls, electric gates with dense vegetation behind them ... It's hard to see from outside what goes on in there. Whereas the houses in Tricase are out in the open, like they're talking to one another.'

'Have you become a poet, Fazio?' Montalbano asked.

Fazio blushed.

'Sometimes,' he confessed.

Having reached the edge of the plateau, they got out of the car. At the bottom of the cliff, the sea foamed white where the waves struck a cluster of rocks, and further down it had completely flooded a small beach. It was an unusual shoreline, with stretches of bristling rocks alternating with flat areas of beach. A solitary villa had been built at the very top of a small promontory. Its vast terrace balcony hung as though suspended over the sea. The stretch of shore below consisted entirely of tall rocks, some of them looking like monoliths, but it had nevertheless been closed off — illegally, of course — to create a private space. There was nothing else to see. They got back in the car.

'Now I'm going to take you to talk to a guy—'

'No,' said the inspector. 'There's no point. You can tell me later what those people said. Let's go back.'

During the entire drive there and the entire drive back, they didn't encounter a single car. And they didn't see any parked, either.

In front of a decidedly luxurious villa, they saw a man sitting on a cane chair, smoking a cigar.

'That gentleman,' said Fazio, 'is one of the two who said they had seen the man in the photograph. He's the villa's caretaker. He told me that about three months ago, he was sitting outside the way he is now, when he saw a car come sputtering up from the left. The car stopped right in front of him and a man got out, the same man as in the photo. He'd run out of petrol. So the caretaker offered to go and get him a canful from the garage outside Montechiaro. When he came back with the petrol, the man gave him a tip of a hundred euro.'

'So he didn't see where the guy came from.'

'No. And he'd never seen him before. As for the other guy that recognized him, I was only able to have a brief discussion with him. He's a fisherman and had a basket full of fish he had to go and sell in Montechiaro. He told me he'd seen the man in the picture about three, four months ago, on the beach.'

'Three or four months ago? But that was the middle of the winter! What was he doing there?'

'That's the same thing the fisherman asked himself. He'd just pulled his boat ashore when he saw the man from the photograph on a rock nearby.'

'On a rock?'

'Yeah, one of those rocks right under the villa with the big terrace.'

'And what was he doing?'

'Nothing. He was looking out at the sea and talking on a mobile phone. But the fisherman got a good look at him, 'cause at one point the man turned around and started glaring at him. He had the impression the guy on the rock was trying to tell him something.'

'Like what?'

'Like get the fuck out of here . . . What do I do now?'

'I don't understand. What are you supposed to do?'

'Should I keep looking, or should I stop?'

'Well, it seems useless to waste any more of your time. You can go back to Vigàta.'

Fazio breathed a sigh of relief. This search hadn't agreed with him from the start.

'You're not coming?'

'I'll be along later. First I need to stop for a few minutes in Montechiaro.'

*

It was a bald-faced lie; he had nothing whatsoever to do in Montechiaro. For a stretch he followed Fazio's car, and then, when he'd lost sight of it, he did a U-turn and drove back in the direction he'd come. Spigonella had made an impression on him. Was it possible there wasn't a living soul besides the cigar-smoking caretaker in that entire residential area? He hadn't seen any dogs, either, or even a single cat turned feral by the seclusion. It was an ideal location for anyone who wanted to do whatever he pleased – like shack up with a woman in secret, set up a gambling house, or organize an orgy or giant snortfest. One needed only take care to cover the windows with shades that didn't let a single ray of light filter out, and nobody would ever know what was going on inside. Every villa had enough space around it for cars to enter and park well inside the gate and walls. Once the gate closed, it was as though those cars had never come.

While driving around, he had an idea. He braked, got out, and started walking, looking absorbed, now and then kicking the little white stones he encountered along the road.

The little boy's long escape, which had begun on the landing wharf in the port of Vigàta, had ended not far from Spigonella. He was almost certain the child was running away from Spigonella when the car ran him down.

The nameless dead man he'd encountered while out for a swim had also been sighted in Spigonella. And in all likelihood he'd been killed in Spigonella. Their two stories seemed to run parallel, even though they weren't supposed to. The inspector recalled the famous expression coined by a politician killed by the Red Brigades: 'parallel convergences'. Was the ultimate point of convergence none other than the ghost town of Spigonella? Why not?

But where to begin? Should he try to find out who owned those villas? This immediately seemed an impossible undertaking. Since every single one of those constructions was strictly unauthorized, there was no point in checking the land registry or town hall. Discouraged, he leaned against an electrical pole. The moment his shoulders touched the wood of the pole, he stepped away as though he'd had a shock. Electricity! Of course! All towns had to have electricity, and therefore the homeowners had to submit signed requests to be hooked up. But his enthusiasm was short-lived. He could already imagine the electrical company's response: since there were no registered streets or street numbers in Spigonella, and since, in short, there was no such place as Spigonella, the electrical bills were sent to the owners' regular residential addresses. Sorting out these owners would surely be a long and arduous process. And were he to ask how long, the answer would be so vague as to be almost poetic. What about trying the telephone company? Right!

Aside from the fact that the phone company's answer would have many points in common with the electrical company's, what about mobile phones? Hadn't one of the witnesses, the fisherman, stated that when he'd seen the unknown dead man, the guy was talking on a mobile phone? Hopeless. No matter which way he turned, he ran into a wall. An idea came to him. He got in the car, turned on the ignition, and drove off. Finding the road wasn't easy. He drove past the same villa two or three times, and then finally, in the distance, saw what he was looking for. The caretaker was still sitting in the same cane chair, the extinguished cigar in his mouth. Montalbano pulled up, got out, and approached the man.

'Good afternoon.'

'If you say so ... Good afternoon.'

'I'm a police inspector.'

'I figured. You came by with the other policeman, the one that showed me the photograph.'

Had a sharp eye, this caretaker.

'I wanted to ask you something.'

'Go right ahead.'

'Do you see many immigrants around here?'

The caretaker gave him an astonished look.

'Immigrants? Sir, around here we don't see no immi-grants, emigrants, or even migrants. All we ever see is the people who live here when they come. Immigrants! Hah!'

'Why does that seem so preposterous to you?'

''Cause around here the private-security car passes every two hours. And those guys ... if they saw an immigrant, they'd kick his arse all the way back to where he came from!'

'So why haven't I seen any of these security officers today?'

'Because today they're on strike for half the day.'

'Thank you.'

'No, thank you for helping make a little of the time go by.'

He got back in the car and left. But when he got to the white-and-red house in front of which he and Fazio had met, he turned around. He knew there was nothing to find there, but he couldn't bring himself to leave that place. He pulled up again at the edge of the cliff. It was getting dark. Against the still luminous sky, the villa with the enormous terrace looked ghostly. Despite the luxurious homes, the well-tended trees rising above the enclosure walls, and the lush greenery everywhere, Spigonella was a wasteland. Of course, all seaside towns, especially those that depend on holiday-makers, seem dead in the off-season. But Spigonella must have been already dead at the moment of its birth. Getting back into his car, this time he finally drove back to Vigàta.

'Marzilla call, Cat?'

'No, Chief, he din't. But Pontius Pilate did.'

'What'd he say?'

'He said he in't gonna make the plane, but tomorrow he can, and so tomorrow afternoon he'll be here in the afternoon.'

The inspector went into his office but didn't sit down. He immediately made a phone call. He wanted to see if there was any chance of doing something that had occurred to him as he was parking the car in front of the police station.

'Signora Albanese? Good evening, how are you? This is Inspector Montalbano. Can you tell me what time your husband will stop fishing today? Ah, he didn't go out today? Is he at home? Could I talk to him? Ciccio, what are you doing at home? A touch of the flu? Feeling any better now? All gone? Good, I'm glad. Listen, I wanted to ask you something ... What's that? Why don't I come by for dinner, so we can talk about it in person? I really don't want to take advantage of you, or put your wife to any trouble ... What was that? Pasta with fresh ricotta? And a second course of whitebait? I'll be there in half an hour.'

*

He was unable to speak for the duration of the meal. From time to time Ciccio Albanese would ask him:

'What was that you wanted to ask me, Inspector?'

But Montalbano didn't even answer, merely rotating the forefinger of his left hand, gesturing 'later, later', since either his mouth was too full or he simply didn't want to open it, lest the air dilute the taste he was jealously guarding between his tongue and palate.

When the coffee was served, he decided it was time to talk about what he wanted, but only after complimenting Albanese's wife on her cooking.

'You were right, Ciccio. The dead man was spotted three months ago at Spigonella. Things must have happened the way you said: first they killed him, then they threw him into the water at Spigonella or nearby. You really are very good, as everyone says.'

Ciccio Albanese absorbed the praise without a blink, as his due.

'What else can I do for you?' was all he said.

Montalbano told him. Albanese thought about it a minute, then turned to his wife.

'Is Tanino in Montelusa or Palermo? Do you know?'

'This morning my sister said he was here.'

Before phoning Montelusa, Albanese felt he needed to explain.

'Tanino is my wife's sister's son. He's studying law in Palermo. His dad has a house in Tricase and Tanino goes there often. He's got a dinghy and likes to scuba dive.'

The phone call took only about five minutes.

'Tanino'll expect you at eight o'clock tomorrow morning. Now let me explain how you get there.'

*

'Fazio? Sorry to bother you at this hour, but the other day, I think I saw one of our men with a small video camera and—'

'Yeah, that was Torrisi, Chief. He just bought it. From Torretta.'

Of course! Torretta must have moved the entire Zanzibar bazaar into the Vigàta police headquarters!

'Send Torrisi right over here to Marinella, with the video camera and anything else I might need to operate it.'

ELEVEN

When he opened the shutters, he took heart. The morning looked happy to be what it was, alive with light and colour. In the shower Montalbano even tried to sing, which he rarely did; being somewhat tone-deaf, however, he merely hummed the tune. Though he wasn't running late, he realized he was hurrying because he was anxious to leave the house and get to Tricase. In the car, in fact, he realized at one point that he was driving too fast. At the Spigonella–Tricase fork, he turned left and, once past the bend, found himself at the mound of gravel. The bouquet of flowers was gone, and there was a labourer filling a wheelbarrow with gravel. A bit further on, two more labourers worked on the road. The few paltry things commemorating the death and life of the little boy had all disappeared. By now his small body must have been buried anonymously in the Montechiaro cemetery. At Tricase he carefully followed the instructions Ciccio Albanese had given him and, when very near the shore, he pulled up in front of a small yellow house. A pleasant-looking kid of about twenty, in shorts and barefoot, stood in the doorway. A rubber dinghy bobbed in the water a short distance away. They shook hands. Tanino gave the inspector a curious look, and only then did Montalbano realize he was decked out like a tourist. In fact, in addition to the video camera in his hand, he had a pair of binoculars slung across his chest.

'Shall we go?' asked the kid.

'Sure. But first I want to undress.'

'Go ahead.'

He went into the house and came back out in a bathing suit. Tanino locked the door and they climbed aboard the dinghy. Only then did the kid ask:

'Where are we going?'

'Your uncle didn't tell you?'

'My uncle only told me to make myself available.'

'I want to shoot some footage of the coast at Spigonella. But I don't want anyone to see us.'

'Who's going to see us, Inspector? At this time of year there isn't a soul in Spigonella.'

'Just do as I say.'

After barely half an hour on the water, Tanino slowed down.

'Down there are the first houses in Spigonella. Is this speed OK for you?'

'Perfect.'

'Should I go a little closer?'

'No.'

Montalbano grabbed the video camera and realized, to his horror, that he didn't know how to use it. The instructions Torretta had given him the night before had turned into a formless mush in his brain.

'*Matre santa!* I can't remember anything!' he groaned.

'Want me to try? I've got one just like it at home.'

They traded places, and the inspector took the tiller, steering with one hand and holding the binoculars to his eyes with the other.

'And this is where Spigonella ends,' Tanino said at a certain point, turning around to face the inspector.

Lost in thought, Montalbano didn't answer. The binoculars dangled from his neck.

'Inspector?'

'Hm?'

'What should we do now?'

'Let's go back. And, if possible, a little closer and a little slower.'

'It's possible.'

'Another thing: when we're in front of the villa with the big terrace, could you zoom in on those rocks in the water below?'

They passed by Spigonella a second time, then left it behind them.

'What next?'

'Are you sure you got some good shots?'

'Cross my heart.'

'OK, then, let's go home. Do you know who owns that villa with the terrace?'

'I do. An American had it built, but that was before I was born.'

'An American?'

'Actually he was the son of a couple that had emigrated from Montechiaro. He came here a few times in the early days, or at least that's what I'm told. Then he never came back. There were rumours he'd been arrested.'

'Here in Sicily?'

'No, in America. For smuggling.'

'Drugs?'

'And cigarettes. People say that for a while he was directing all the traffic in the Mediterranean from here.'

'Have you ever seen those rocks in front of the house from up close?'

'Around here, Inspector, everybody minds his own business.'

'Has anyone been living in the villa recently?'

'Not recently, no. But there was somebody there last year.'

'So they rent it out?'

'I guess.'

'Do they use an agency?'

'Inspector, I have no idea. If you want, I can try to find out.'

'No, that's all right, thanks. You've gone to enough trouble as it is.'

*

When he pulled into the main square in Montechiaro, the town clock rang eleven thirty. He stopped the car, got out, and headed for a glass door with the words Estate Agent over it. Inside there was only a pretty, polite girl.

'No, we don't handle the villa you're talking about.'

'Do you know who does?'

'No. You see, the owners of these luxury villas very rarely use agencies, at least not around here.'

'So how do they rent them, then?'

'You know, they're all rich and they all know each other . . . They just get the word out in their circles . . .'

Crooks also get the word out in their circles, thought the inspector.

Meanwhile the girl was looking at him and noticed the binoculars and video camera.

'Are you a tourist?'

'How could you tell?' said Montalbano.

*

After that jaunt over the waves he felt irresistibly hungry, his appetite swelling inside him like a river in spate. Though the surest course would have been to head straight to the Trattoria Da Enzo, he had to take his chances with what awaited him in the refrigerator or the oven in Marinella, since he needed to view what they'd filmed right away. As soon as he got home, he dashed into the kitchen, anxious to see what Adelina's imagination had cooked up for him. In the oven he found rabbit *alla cacciatora*, as unexpected as it was ardently desired. While warming it up, he grabbed the phone.

'Torrisi? Montalbano here.'

'Everything go all right, Inspector?'

'I think so. Could you pop over to my place in about an hour?'

When eating alone, one indulges oneself in ways one would never dare in the company of others. Some sit at the table in their underwear, others stuff themselves in bed or set up in front of the TV. Often the inspector allowed himself the pleasure of eating with his hands. Which is what he did with the rabbit *alla cacciatora*. Afterwards he had to spend half an hour scrubbing his hands under the kitchen tap to wash off the grease and the smell.

He went to answer the door. It was Torrisi.

'Let me see what we filmed,' said the inspector.

'Here's how you do it, Chief. Watch. You flip this switch and . . .'

He performed the procedure as he spoke, but Montalbano wasn't even listening. He was utterly hopeless in these matters. The first images Tanino had filmed appeared on the television screen.

'What beautiful shots, Inspector!' Torrisi said with admiration. 'You're really good, you know. After only one technical lesson last night...'

'Well,' Montalbano said modestly, 'it wasn't hard...'

In the footage shot on the first run, the rocks below the villa looked like a bottom row of uneven teeth in a giant mouth, one jutting out, another recessed, one shorter than the rest, one longer, one slanting crosswise, another standing upright. When filmed on the return run, the same mouth of rocks appeared to be missing a tooth, revealing a gap that was not very wide, just enough to allow a dinghy or small motorboat to pass through.

'Stop there.'

Montalbano studied the image carefully. Something about that gap looked odd to him, as though the sea hesitated slightly before entering. In spots, it even looked like it wanted to turn back.

'Can you enlarge?'

'No, Chief.'

When Tanino stopped zooming, one saw the very steep staircase, carved directly into the rock, leading from the villa to the small, natural harbour formed by the rocks.

'Go back a little, please.'

This time he noticed a tall wire fence welded to some metal poles planted in the rocks, preventing anyone from climbing up and seeing what was going on inside the little harbour. Thus not only was the villa built without authorization, but its owners had illegally interrupted the shoreline.

There was no way to walk along the water's edge there, not even by climbing the rocks, since at a certain point one's path was blocked by an insurmountable barrier of wire fencing. Yet even on this second viewing, he couldn't figure out why the sea acted so strangely in front of that missing tooth.

'Good enough, Torrisi. Thanks. You can take back your video camera.'

'There is a way to enlarge the image you wanted, Chief. I could print out a copy of the still and give it to Catarella, who then could scan—'

'Fine, fine, you take care of it,' Montalbano cut him off.

'My compliments again on the beautiful shots,' said Torrisi as he went out.

'Thanks,' said the inspector, with the cheek he was able to summon in certain situations. The usurper didn't even blush.

*

'Cat, any news from Marzilla?'

'No sir, Chief. But I wanted a tell you that a litter came this morning, addrissed to you poissonally in poisson.'

The plainest of envelopes, with no letterhead. The inspector opened it and pulled out a newspaper clipping. He looked inside the envelope but found nothing else. There was a short article dated Cosenza, 11 March. The headline said: FUGITIVE ERRERA'S BODY FOUND. It said:

Yesterday morning around 6.00 a.m., Antonio Jacopino, a
shepherd, was horrified to discover the remains of a human
body when crossing the railway line near Paganello with his
flock. Preliminary investigations by the police, who
promptly rushed to the scene, point to an apparent mishap.
The man is believed to have slid down the embankment,
made slippery by recent rainfall, as the 11:00 pm express was
passing by on its way to Cosenza. In their statement to
police, the conductors stated they noticed nothing unusual
when passing that spot. Authorities were able to identify
the victim from the documents in his wallet and a wedding
ring. His name was Ernesto Errera, a fugitive from justice,
convicted by the Court of Cosenza for armed robbery. He
had lately been rumoured to be active in Brindisi, having
taken an interest in trafficking illegal immigrants and working in close contact with the Albanian mafia.

That was all. No signature, no note of explanation. He
looked at the postmark: Cosenza. What the hell did it
mean? Perhaps there was an explanation. Maybe it was
some kind of internal vendetta. In all probability, his
colleague Vattiato had mentioned how Montalbano had
made a fool of himself when he called up to say he'd found
the body of someone already dead and buried, and one of
the people present, apparently someone not too fond of
Vattiato, had decided to send the inspector the clipping on
the sly. Because that short article, if read properly, somewhat
undermined the certainty of Vattiato's position. The anonymous sender of that clipping was actually posing a very
simple question: if the man torn to pieces by that train was

identified as Ernesto Errera solely on the basis of his
identification papers and a wedding ring, how could anyone
be absolutely certain that those mortal remains really
belonged to Errera? Might it not have been Errera himself
who killed someone bearing a vague resemblance to him,
put his own wallet in the man's pocket, his wedding ring
on his finger, and then laid him down in the tracks in such
a way as to make him unrecognizable once the train had
run over him? And why would he have done this? For
obvious reasons: so the police and carabinieri would stop
looking for him, and he could therefore operate in relative
peace in Brindisi.

Yet no sooner had the inspector made these conjectures
than they seemed like something out of a novel. He called
Augello. Mimì came in with a dark face.

'Not feeling well?'

'Leave me alone, Salvo. I was up all night helping Beba.
This has been a very difficult pregnancy. What did you
want?'

'Some advice. But I want you to hear something first.
Catarella!'

'Yer orders, Chief!'

'Cat, tell Inspector Augello your theory about Errera,
the same way you told it to me.'

Catarella puffed himself up.

'I tole the Chief Inspector as how maybe, just maybe, it
was possible the dead guy came back to life and then went
back to death in the water.'

'Thanks, Cat. You can go now.'

Mimì was looking at him dumbfounded.

'Well?' the inspector prodded him.

'Listen, Salvo. Until a minute ago, I thought your resignation would be a tragedy for all of us. But now, seeing your mental condition, I'm thinking the sooner you go, the better. What is this? So now you're starting to take the nonsense that passes between Catarella's ears seriously? Back to death in the water?'

Without saying a word, Montalbano handed him the newspaper clipping.

Mimì read it through twice. Then he set it down on the desk.

'What do you think it means?' he asked.

'That someone wanted to let me know that there's a chance – a remote one, admittedly – that the body buried in Cosenza is not Ernesto Errera's,' said Montalbano.

'The piece you had me read,' said Mimì, 'was written by a reporter two or three days after the body's remains were found. And it doesn't say whether our Cosenza colleagues did any further, more serious investigation that could have led to a more definite identification. Dental checks, fingerprints, that kind of thing. Which they surely must have done. And if you start digging and trying to find out more about the case, you risk falling into the trap they've set for you.'

'What are you talking about?!'

'Do you have any idea who sent you the clipping?'

'Maybe somebody from Cosenza Police who overheard Vattiato ragging me and wanted to give me a chance—'

'Salvo, do you know Vattiato?'

'Not very well. He's a surly—'

'I worked with him before coming here. He's a son of a bitch.'

'But why would he send me the article?'

'To arouse your curiosity and make you start asking questions about Errera. So he can have the whole police department of Cosenza laughing at you.'

Montalbano stood up halfway out of his chair, searched through the papers scattered helter-skelter over his desk, and found Errera's dossier and photos.

'Have another look at these, Mimì.'

Holding the dossier with Errera's photo in his left hand, Mimì picked up, one by one, the computerized reconstructions of the dead man's face with his right, comparing each of them closely with the mug shot. Then he shook his head.

'I'm sorry, Salvo. My opinion hasn't changed. Those are two different people, even though they do look rather alike. Have you anything else to tell me?'

'No,' the inspector said brusquely.

Augello became irritated.

'Salvo, I've got enough problems of my own to put me on edge. I don't need you creating more.'

'Explain.'

'You want an explanation? You're pissed off because I

171

keep insisting that your corpse is not Errera. You're really something, you know. Am I supposed to say, yes, they're the same person, just to make you happy?'

He went out, slamming the door behind him.

*

Not five minutes later, the same door flew open, crashed against the wall, and, on the rebound, closed again.

'Sorry, Chief,' said Catarella's voice from behind the door.

The door then began to open very slowly, just enough to allow Catarella to slide through.

'Chief, I brought you the ting Torrisi gave me which he said you was poissonally intristed in.'

It was a greatly enlarged image of a detail of the rocks below the villa in Spigonella.

'It can't come out no better than 'at, Chief.'

'Thanks, Cat, you did an excellent job.'

A glance sufficed to convince him he'd been right.

Between the two tall rocks forming the narrow entrance of the tiny natural harbour, there was a straight, dark line, barely an inch above the water, against which the surf broke. It must have been an iron barrier that could be operated from inside the villa to prevent outsiders from entering the little harbour with any sort of craft. This might not indicate anything suspicious, of course; it might only mean that unannounced visitors were unwelcome. Studying the rocks more closely, he noticed something else that piqued his curiosity, about three feet above the water. He looked and looked until the image began to blur before his eyes.

'Catarella!'

'Yessir, Chief!'

'Get Torretta to lend you a magnifying glass.'

'Right away, Chief.'

He'd guessed right. Catarella returned with a big magnifying glass and handed it to the inspector.

'Thanks, you can go now. And close the door behind you.'

He wouldn't want to be caught by Mimì or Fazio in a pose typical of Sherlock Holmes.

With the help of the glass, he managed to figure out what he was looking at. There were two small signal lights which when illuminated at night or in conditions of poor visibility would precisely mark the boundaries of the entrance, allowing anyone manoeuvring a craft to enter without risk of crashing into the rocks. They must certainly have been installed by the villa's original owner, the American smuggler, and the whole set-up must have been very useful to him. Still, subsequent tenants had kept it in working order. He pondered this a long time. Slowly, he began to think he ought perhaps to go and take another, closer look – from the sea, if possible. And, most importantly, on the sly, without telling anyone.

He glanced at his watch. Ingrid would be there at any moment. He took his wallet out of his pocket to see if he had enough money for dinner. Catarella stuck his head inside the door and said, panting:

'Ahh, Chief! Miss Ingrid's ousside, waiting for you!'

*

Ingrid wanted the inspector to get in her car.

'With yours we'll never get there, and it's pretty far.'

'Where on earth are you taking me?'

'You'll see. You can break the monotony of your fish dishes once in a while, can't you?'

Between Ingrid's chatter and the speed she maintained, it didn't seem like they'd been driving long when the car pulled up in front of a farmhouse in the open country. Was it really a restaurant, or had Ingrid made a mistake? When he saw a dozen or so parked cars, he felt reassured. Once inside, Ingrid greeted all present and they all greeted her. She was one of the family. The manager came rushing over.

'Salvo, will you have what I'm going to have?' Ingrid asked.

The inspector thus enjoyed a dish of ditalini in a sauce of fresh and properly salted ricotta, with pecorino and black pepper on top. The dish cried out for wine, a demand that was amply fulfilled. For the second course they stuffed themselves with *costi 'mbriachi*, that is, 'drunken' pork ribs drowning in wine and tomato concentrate. When it was time to pay the bill, the inspector blanched: he'd left his wallet on his desk. Ingrid took care of it. On the drive back, the car did a few waltz-like turns. As they approached the police station, Montalbano asked Ingrid to stop so he could get his wallet.

'I'll come in with you,' she said. 'I've never seen where you work.'

They went into his office. The inspector walked over to his desk, Ingrid following behind. As he grabbed the wallet, Ingrid noticed the photos on the table and picked one up.

'Why do you have pictures of Ninì on your desk?'

TWELVE

For an instant everything stopped; for an instant, even the confused background noise of the world vanished. Even a fly that was decidedly aiming for the inspector's nose froze, suspended in air, wings spread. Getting no answer to her question, Ingrid looked up. Montalbano looked like a statue, wallet half-inserted in his jacket pocket, mouth hanging open, eyes staring at Ingrid.

'Why do you have all those pictures of Ninì?' she asked again, picking up the other photos on the desk.

A kind of furious southwester, meanwhile, was blasting through all the twists and turns of the inspector's brain, and he couldn't get hold of himself. What?! They'd searched everywhere, phoned Cosenza, combed the archives, questioned potential witnesses, explored Spigonella by land and sea in the hopes of giving that corpse a name, and along came Ingrid, cool as a cucumber, actually calling it by a nickname?

'D-d-d ... y-y-y ... ouuu ... nnn—'

Montalbano was struggling to get out the question, 'Do

you know him?' but Ingrid misunderstood and interrupted him.

'D'Iunio, exactly,' she said. 'I believe I already mentioned him to you once.'

True enough. She'd talked about him the evening they'd downed a bottle of whisky on the veranda. She said she'd had an affair with this D'Iunio, but they'd broken it off because ... Because why?

'Why did you break up?'

'I broke off the affair. There was something about him that made me uneasy ... I was always on my guard ... I could never relax with him ... Even though there wasn't really any reason ...'

'Did he make unusual ... demands on you?'

'In bed?'

'Yes.'

Ingrid shrugged. 'Well, no more unusual than any other man.'

Why did he feel an absurd twinge of jealousy upon hearing these words?

'So, what was it, then?'

'Just a feeling, Salvo. I can't really explain it ...'

'What did he say he did for a living?'

'He'd been captain of an oil tanker ... Then he came into some kind of inheritance ... In reality, he didn't do anything.'

'How did you meet him?'

Ingrid laughed.

'By chance. At a petrol station. There was a long queue, and we started talking.'

'Where did you normally get together?'

'In a place called Spigonella. Do you know where it is?'

'Yeah, I know it.'

'Excuse me, Salvo, but are you interrogating me?'

'I'd say so.'

'Why?'

'I'll explain later.'

'Would you mind if we continued somewhere else?'

'Why, don't you like it here?'

'No. In here, the way you're asking me those questions ... you seem like a different person.'

'A different person?'

'Yes, a different person, someone I don't know. Could we go to your place?'

'If you like. But no whisky. At least not before we've finished.'

'Yes, sir, Mr Inspector.'

*

They drove to Marinella in separate cars, and naturally Ingrid got there long before he did.

Montalbano went and opened the French windows giving onto the veranda.

It was a very soft night, perhaps a little too soft. The air smelt of brine and mist. The inspector took a deep breath, his lungs enjoying the sweetness.

'Shall we go and sit on the veranda?' Ingrid suggested.

'No, it's better inside.'

They sat down across from each other at the dining room table. Ingrid stared at him, looking perplexed. The inspector set the envelope with D'Iunio's photos, which he'd brought from the station, down on the table beside him.

'Want to tell me why you're so interested in Nini?'

'No.'

Ingrid felt hurt, and Montalbano noticed.

'If I told you, it would very probably influence your answers. You said you called him Nini. Is that a diminutive for Antonio?'

'No. Ernesto.'

Was it a coincidence? People who change identities often keep the initials of their first and last names. Did the fact that both D'Iunio and Errera were called Ernesto mean they were the same person? Better go at it slowly, one step at a time.

'Was he Sicilian?'

'He never told me where he was from. Except he once said he'd been married to a girl from Catanzaro who died two years after they were married.'

'Catanzaro, he said?'

Ingrid seemed to hesitate, sticking the tip of her tongue between her lips.

'Or was it Cosenza?' Adorable wrinkles appeared on her forehead. 'My mistake. I'm sure he said Cosenza.'

That made two! The late Mr Ernesto D'Iunio kept

picking up points of resemblance to the equally late Mr Ernesto Errera. Without warning, Montalbano got up and kissed Ingrid on the corner of her mouth. She gave him a quizzical look.

'Do you always do that when the person you're questioning gives you the answer you want to hear?'

'Yes, especially when it's a man. Tell me something. Did your Ninì walk with a limp?'

'Not always. Only in bad weather. But you could hardly tell.'

Dr Pasquano had been right. Except that there was no way to know whether Errera also limped or not.

'How long did your affair last?'

'Not very long, a month and a half, maybe a little longer. But . . .'

'But?'

'It was very intense.'

Another twinge of groundless jealousy.

'And when did it end?'

'About two months ago.'

Shortly before somebody killed him, therefore.

'Tell me exactly what you did when you broke it off with him.'

'I called him on his mobile in the morning to tell him I was coming to see him that same evening in Spigonella.'

'Did you always meet in the evening?'

'Yes, late in the evening.'

'So you never, say, went out to eat?'

'No, we never met anywhere but in Spigonella. It was as though he didn't want to be seen, either with me or without me. That was another thing that bothered me.'

'Go on.'

'Anyway, I called him to say I'd be at his place that evening. But he said there was no way he could see me. Somebody had come unexpectedly, and he needed to talk to this person. The same thing had already happened twice before. So we arranged to meet the following night. Except that I never went. By my own choice.'

'Ingrid, honestly, I don't understand why, all of a sudden, you—'

'I'll try to explain, Salvo. Whenever I arrived there in my car, the front gate would be open and I would drive up the driveway to the villa. Then there was a second gate, which would also be open. While I pulled into the garage, Ninì, in the dark, would go and close the gates. Then we would go up the stairs—'

'What stairs?'

'The villa has two storeys, right? Ninì was renting the upstairs, which you could enter by an external staircase on the side of the house.'

'Let me get this straight. He wasn't renting the whole villa?'

'No, just the upstairs.'

'And the two floors were not connected?'

'Yes, they were. Or at least that's what Ninì said. There

was a door that led to an internal staircase, but the door was locked and the landlord had the key.'

'So you got to know only the upper floor?'

'Right. As I was saying, we would go up the stairs and straight into the bedroom. Nini was a maniac. Before we could ever turn on a light in a room, he had to make sure it couldn't be seen from outside. Not only were all the shutters closed, but there were heavy curtains over all the windows.'

'Go on.'

'We would get undressed and start making love.'

This time it wasn't a twinge, but an out-and-out stab wound.

'Who knows why I started having second thoughts about our affair after I couldn't see him that time? The first thing I noticed was that I had never felt like sleeping with Nini — I mean, spending the night there with him. After making love, I would just lie there, smoking the customary cigarette, staring at the ceiling. Him too. We never talked. We had nothing to say to each other. And those bars over the windows—'

'Bars?'

'Over all the windows. Even on the ground floor. I used to see them even when I couldn't see them, when the curtains were drawn ... They made me feel like I was in some kind of prison ... Sometimes he would get up and go and talk over the radio ...'

'Over the radio? What kind of radio?'

'A ham radio. It was his hobby, he told me. He said

that when he used to sail the seas the radio always kept him company, and ever since ... He had a huge set-up in the living room.'

'Did you ever hear what he said?'

'Yes, but I didn't understand ... He often spoke in Arabic or some similar language. After a while I would get dressed and leave. Anyway, that day I started asking myself some questions, and I decided our affair was meaningless, or that, in any case, it had gone on too long. And so I didn't go to see him.'

'Did he have your mobile-phone number?'

'Yes.'

'And he used to call you?'

'Of course. He would call when he wanted to tell me I should come a little later than planned, or a little earlier.'

'Weren't you surprised that he didn't come looking for you when you never showed up for your appointment?'

'To be honest, yes. But when he didn't call, I decided it was better that way.'

'Listen, I want you to try hard to remember. When you were with him there, did you ever hear any noises in the rest of the house?'

'What do you mean, in the rest of the house? Do you mean the other rooms?'

'No, I meant on the ground floor.'

'What kind of noises?'

'I dunno, voices, sounds ... a car pulling up ...'

'No. The downstairs was empty.'

'Did he get a lot of phone calls?'

'When we were together, he would turn off his mobile phones.'

'How many did he have?'

'Two. One was a satellite phone. Whenever he turned them on, someone would call almost immediately.'

'Did he always speak in Arabic or whatever that language was?'

'No, sometimes he'd speak Italian. And in that case he would go into another room. But it's not like I really cared to know what he was saying.'

'How did he explain them?'

'Explain what?'

'All those phone calls.'

'Why should he explain them?'

True enough, again.

'Do you know if he had any friends in this area?'

'I certainly never saw any. I don't think so. It suited him just fine, not having any friends.'

'Why's that?'

'One of the few times he told me about himself, he said that on his last voyage, his tanker had caused a huge environmental disaster. There was a lawsuit still pending, and the shipping company had advised him to disappear for a while. Which explained everything: the secluded villa, why he always stayed home, and so on.'

Even assuming everything he told Ingrid was true, thought the inspector, it still didn't explain why D'Iunio—

Errera had died the way he did. Was one to think that his shipping firm, to keep him quiet, had ordered him killed? Come on. There certainly were dark motives behind the murder and, according to Ingrid's description of him, he wasn't a man with nothing to hide. But these dark motives lay elsewhere.

'I think I've earned a little whisky, Mr Inspector,' Ingrid said at this point.

Montalbano got up and opened the drinks cabinet. Luckily Adelina had remembered to re-stock. There was a brand-new bottle. He went in the kitchen to get two glasses, returned, sat down, and filled the glasses halfway. They both wanted it neat. Ingrid took her glass, raised it, and eyed the inspector.

'He's dead, isn't he?'

'Yes.'

'Murdered, right? If not, you wouldn't be handling the case.'

Montalbano nodded yes.

'When did it happen?'

'I believe he never called you after you failed to show up because he was no longer in any condition to do so.'

'He was already dead?'

'I don't know if they killed him immediately or kept him prisoner a long time.'

'Killed him . . . how?'

'Drowned him.'

'How did you find him?'

'He found me, actually.'

'I don't understand.'

'Remember when you saw me naked on TV?'

'Yes.'

'The dead body I bumped into on my swim was his.'

Only then did Ingrid bring the glass to her lips, and she didn't lower it until there wasn't a drop of whisky left in it. Then she got up, went to the veranda, and stepped outside. Montalbano took his first sip and lit a cigarette. Ingrid came back inside and went into the bathroom. She returned after washing her face, sat back down, and refilled her glass.

'Have you any more questions?'

'A few more. Is there anything of yours at the villa in Spigonella?'

'What do you mean?'

'Did you leave anything of yours there?'

'Like what?'

'How should I know? A change of clothes . . .'

'Panties?'

'Uh . . .'

'No, there's nothing of mine there. As I said, I never felt like spending the whole night there with him. Why do you ask?'

'Because, sooner or later, we'll have to search the villa.'

'Don't worry about that. Any other questions? I'm feeling a little tired.'

Montalbano pulled the photos out of his pocket and handed them to Ingrid.

'Which one looks most like him?'

'But aren't these pictures of him?'

'They're computer composites. His face was very badly deteriorated, unrecognizable.'

Ingrid studied them, then chose the one with the moustache.

'This one,' she said. 'But . . .'

'But?'

'Two things are wrong. His moustache was a lot longer and had a different shape, kind of a handlebar moustache . . .'

'And the other thing?'

'The nose. The nostrils were wider.'

Montalbano took the dossier out of the envelope.

'As in this shot?'

'That's him, all right,' said Ingrid. 'Even without the moustache.'

There was no longer any doubt: D'Iunio and Errera were the same person. Catarella's wacky theory had proved true.

Montalbano stood up and held his hand out to Ingrid, making her get up. When she was fully erect, he embraced her.

'Thanks,' he said.

Ingrid looked at him.

'Is that all?' she said.

'Let's take the bottle and glasses out on the veranda,' said the inspector. 'Now the fun begins.'

✳

They settled onto the bench very close to each other. The night now smelt of brine, mint, whisky, and apricot, which was exactly what Ingrid's skin smelt like. It was a blend not even a prize *parfumeur* could have invented.

They didn't speak. They were happy just the way they were. Her third glass Ingrid left half full.

'Do you mind if I lie down on your bed?' she murmured suddenly.

'Don't you want to go home?'

'I don't feel up to driving.'

'I'll take you home in my car. You can come and pick it up—'

'I don't want to go home. But if you really don't want me to stay here, I'll just lie down for a few minutes. Then I'll go. OK?'

'OK.'

Ingrid stood up, kissed him on the forehead, and went inside. *I don't want to go home*, she'd said. What did Ingrid's and her husband's house represent for her? Perhaps a bed even more alien than the one she was presently lying in? And if she'd had a child, would her home have seemed different to her, warmer, more welcoming? Poor woman! How much loneliness and melancholy might she be hiding under her apparently superficial joie de vivre? He felt a new emotion towards Ingrid well up inside him, a kind of heartbreaking tenderness. He swallowed a few more sips of whisky and, as a cool wind had started to blow, went inside with the bottle and glasses. He glanced over at the bedroom. Ingrid was sleeping with her clothes on, having removed only her shoes. He sat back down at the table. He wanted to let her sleep another ten minutes or so.

Meanwhile let's do a brief review of the previous episodes, he said to himself.

Ernesto Errera is an habitual offender, born, perhaps, in Cosenza, and in any case operating around there. He has a fine curriculum vitae that ranges from breaking and entering to armed robbery. A wanted man, he becomes a fugitive from justice. Up to this point, no different from hundreds and hundreds of other crooks just like him. Then at some point Errera resurfaces in Brindisi.

He seems to have established excellent relations with the Albanian mafia and is now involved in illegal immigration. But how? In what capacity? We don't know.

On the morning of 11 March of last year, a shepherd from the Cosenza area finds a man's mangled body on the railway line. In an unfortunate accident, the poor bastard slipped and wasn't able to get out of the way of the coming train. He is so badly mutilated that the only way to identify him is from the documents in his wallet and a wedding ring. His wife has him buried in the Cosenza cemetery. A few months later, Errera turns up again in Spigonella, Sicily. Except now his name is Ernesto D'Iunio, a widower and former captain of an oil tanker. He leads an apparently solitary life, though he has frequent telephone contact and often talks over a two-way radio. One unfortunate day somebody drowns him and lets him rot. Then they put him out to sea. While sailing the seas, the corpse ends up crossing paths with none other than himself.

First question: what the hell was Mr Errera doing in Spigonella after having himself officially declared dead? Second question: who had made sure that he was not only officially but concretely dead, and why?

It was time to wake Ingrid up. He went into the bedroom. She had undressed and got under the covers. She was sleeping soundly. Montalbano didn't have the heart to wake her. He went in the bathroom and then slipped ever so gently between the sheets. The apricot scent of Ingrid's skin immediately assailed his nostrils; it was so strong he began to feel slightly dizzy. He closed his eyes. Ingrid moved in her sleep and stretched out one leg, placing her calf against Montalbano's. A few minutes later, she got more comfortable. Now her whole leg was resting against him, imprisoning him. Some words came back to him, words he had memorized for a play as a teenager: *There are ... certain good apricots ... that break down the middle ... press them lengthwise with your fingers ... and they open like two succulent lips ...*

Bathed in sweat, the inspector counted to ten and, with a series of almost imperceptible movements, managed to free himself, got out of bed, and, cursing the saints, went to lie down on the sofa.

Jesus Christ! Not even Saint Anthony would have made it through that one!

THIRTEEN

He woke up aching all over. For some time now, sleeping on the sofa meant getting up the next morning with broken bones. On the dining room table was a little note from Ingrid.

Since you're sleeping like a little angel, I've gone to my house to take a shower so I won't wake you up. Kisses, Ingrid. Call me.

He was headed for the bathroom when the phone rang. He glanced at his watch: barely eight o'clock.

'Inspector, I need to see you.'

He didn't recognize the voice.

'Who is this?'

'Marzilla, Inspector.'

'Come to the station.'

'No, not the station. They might see me. I'll come to your place, now that you're alone.'

How the hell did he know that first he had company and now he was alone? Was he hiding somewhere nearby, spying on him?

'Where are you, anyway?'

'In Marinella, Inspector. Practically outside your door. When I saw the woman come out, I called.'

'Wait just a minute and I'll let you in.'

He quickly washed his face and went to open the door. Marzilla, who was leaning against the door as if to take shelter from non-existent rain, came inside, sidestepping the inspector. As he passed, Montalbano got a whiff of rancid sweat. Standing in the middle of the room and panting as if he'd just run a great distance, Marzilla was even paler than before and wild-eyed, his hair sticking straight up.

'I'm scared to death, Inspector.'

'Is there going to be another arrival?'

'Several, and all at the same time.'

'When?'

'The day after tomorrow, at night.'

'Where?'

'They didn't say. But they did let me know that it's going to be a big deal, even though I won't be involved.'

'So why are you afraid? You've got nothing to do with it.'

'Because the person I mentioned, who told me about the arrivals, also told me to call in sick today, so I can be at his disposal.'

'Did he let you know what he wants?'

'Yessir. At ten thirty tonight, I'm supposed to drive a fast car – which they're going to leave in front of my house – to a place near Capo Russello, pick up some people, then drop them off where they tell me to.'

'So, for now, you don't know where you're supposed to take them.'

'No sir. They'll tell me after they get in the car.'

'What time was it when you got the call?'

'Very early this morning, before six. I tried to refuse, Inspector, you've got to believe me. I explained that as long as it involved the ambulance, OK . . . But he wouldn't take no for an answer. He repeatedly said that if I didn't obey, or if something went wrong, he would have me killed.'

He started crying and collapsed into a chair. Montalbano found his tears unbearable, obscene. This man was a piece of shit. A piece of shit quivering like a bowl of jelly. The inspector had to restrain himself from jumping on him and rearranging his face into a bloody mass of skin, flesh, and bones.

'What should I do, Inspector? What should I do?'

Fear had turned his voice into the squawk of a strangled rooster.

'What they told you to do. But the minute they leave the car in front of your place, you have to tell me the model, colour, and, if possible, the licence-plate number. Now get the hell out of here. The more you blubber, the more I feel like kicking your teeth in.'

Never, even if the guy were dying before his eyes, would he forgive him for the shot he had given the little boy in the ambulance. Marzilla sprang to his feet in terror and ran to the door.

'Wait. First tell me exactly where you're meeting those people.'

Marzilla explained. Montalbano didn't really understand, but since he remembered that Catarella had once told him he had a brother who lived in that area, he decided to ask him later on. Marzilla then said:

'What do you intend to do?'

'What do *I* intend to do? You just call me tonight when you've finished, and tell me where you've taken those people and what they're like.'

✳

He resolved – while shaving – not to inform anyone at headquarters of what Marzilla had just told him. After all, the investigation into the little boy's murder was an entirely personal matter, a debt he'd incurred which he was convinced would be very hard, if not impossible, to pay off. Still, he was going to need at least a little help. Among other things, Marzilla had told him they were going to leave a fast car parked in front of his place. Which meant that he, Montalbano, wasn't up to the task. Given his meagre abilities behind the wheel, he would never manage to keep up with Marzilla, who would certainly be asked to drive fast. He had an idea, which he immediately dismissed. Stubbornly, the idea came back to him, and just as stubbornly, he dismissed it again. The idea resurfaced a third time as he was drinking a last coffee before going out. And this time he gave in.

'Hullo? Who 'peakin?'

'This is Inspector Montalbano. Is Signora Ingrid there?'

'You wett, I go see.'

'Salvo! What is it?'

'I need you again.'

'You're insatiable! Wasn't last night enough for you?' said Ingrid, teasing.

'No.'

'Well, if you really can't hold out any longer, I'll be right over.'

'No, there's no need for you to come right now. If you don't have any other engagements, could you be here around nine tonight?'

'Yes.'

'And, listen, have you got another car?'

'I could take my husband's. Why?'

'Yours attracts too much attention. Is your husband's a fast car?'

'Yes.'

'See you tonight, then. Thanks.'

'Wait. In what role?'

'I don't understand.'

'Yesterday I came to your place as a witness. And tonight?'

'Tonight you'll be deputy sheriff. I'll give you a star.'

*

'Chief, Marzilla din't call!' said Catarella, jumping to his feet.

'Thanks, Cat. But stay on the alert, I mean it. Could you send in Inspector Augello and Fazio?'

As he'd decided, he would tell them only about the swimming corpse. Mimì was the first to come in.

'How's Beba?'

'Better. We were finally able to get a little sleep last night.'

Then Fazio appeared.

'I have to tell you,' the inspector began, 'that, entirely by chance, I've managed to identify the drowned man. You, Fazio, did a great job, finding out that he'd recently been spotted in Spigonella. That's where he lived. He'd rented the villa with the big terrace overlooking the sea. D'you remember it, Fazio?'

'Of course.'

'He said he was captain of an oil tanker, and went by the name of Ernesto – "Ninì" to friends – D'Iunio.'

'Why? What was his real name?' asked Augello.

'Ernesto Errera.'

'*Madunnuzza santa!*' said Fazio.

'Like the guy in Cosenza?' asked Mimì again.

'Exactly. They were the same person. Sorry to say, Mimì, but Catarella was right.'

'I want to know how you arrived at this conclusion,' Mimì insisted coldly.

Apparently he was finding the news hard to swallow.

'I didn't arrive at it myself. My friend Ingrid did.'

And he told them the whole story. When he had

finished speaking, Mimì put his head in his hands and shook it at intervals.

'Jesus . . . Jesus . . .' he said softly.

'Why are you so surprised, Mimì?'

'I'm not so surprised by the thing in itself, but by the fact that we were breaking our heads over it when Catarella had come to the right conclusion long before.'

'Then you've never understood just who Catarella is,' said the inspector.

'I guess not. Who is he?'

'Catarella's a little kid, a child inside a grown man's body. And so he reasons like someone barely seven years old.'

'So?'

'What I mean is that Catarella has the kinds of fantasies, brainstorms, and bright ideas a little kid does. And being a little kid, he says what he's thinking, he doesn't hold back. And often he's right on the mark. Because reality, when seen through our eyes, is one thing, but when seen through a child's eyes, it's something else.'

'So, to conclude, what are we going to do?' Fazio cut in.

'That's what I'm asking you,' said Montalbano.

'Chief, I'd like to say something, if Inspector Augello doesn't mind. I want to say that this whole business is not so simple. As things now stand, this murder victim – call him D'Iunio or Errera, it makes no difference – has never been officially declared a murder victim, either by the police or the courts. He's still considered dead by accidental drowning. So my question is: on what grounds do we open a case file and continue the investigation?'

The inspector thought about this a moment.

'We use the old anonymous phone-call trick,' he decided.

Augello and Fazio looked at him questioningly.

'It always works. Don't worry, I've used it before.'

He took out the photo of Errera with a moustache and handed it to Fazio.

'Take this immediately to the Free Channel. I want you to hand it to Nicolò Zito in person. Tell him I need an urgent phone call in this morning's newscast. He should say that Ernesto D'Iunio's family are distraught because they've had no news of him in over two months. Now go.'

Without a peep, Fazio got up and left. Montalbano looked keenly at Augello, as if he'd just noticed at that moment that Mimì was sitting right in front of him. Augello, who knew that look, began to squirm in his chair.

'Salvo, what the hell are you cooking up?'

'How's Beba?'

Mimì gave him a dismayed look.

'You already asked me that, Salvo. She's better.'

'So she's able to make a phone call.'

'Of course. To whom?'

'To the public prosecutor, Tommaseo.'

'And what's she supposed to say to him?'

'I want her to perform a little drama. Half an hour

after Zito broadcasts the photograph on TV, I want Beba to make an anonymous call to Prosecutor Tommaseo and to tell him, in a hysterical voice, that she's seen the man in the photo. She recognizes him perfectly, there is no doubt in her mind.'

'What? Where?' asked Mimì, annoyed and obviously not keen on getting Beba mixed up in the case.

'OK, she has to tell him that about two months ago, when she was sitting in her car in Spigonella, she saw the guy in the photo being badly beaten up by two men. At a certain point he managed to break free and started coming towards Beba's car, when he was caught again by the other two and dragged away.'

'And what was Beba doing in her car?'

'Lewd things with a man.'

'Come on! Beba will never say anything like that! And I don't like it either!'

'And yet it's essential! You know what Tommaseo's like, don't you? Tommaseo lives for these sex stories. It's just the bait we need for him, and he'll bite, just you wait and see. In fact, if Beba can make up a few particularly sordid details—'

'Have you gone insane?'

'Just some little thing . . .'

'Salvo, you're sick in the head!'

'Why are you getting angry? I just meant any old bullshit, like saying that they couldn't intervene because they were both naked—'

'OK, OK. Then what?'

'Then, when Tommaseo calls you, you say—'

'Excuse me, but why would Tommaseo call me instead of you?'

'Because I won't be in this afternoon. I want you to tell him that we already have a lead, have got the missing-person report in hand, and we need a blank search warrant.'

'Blank?!'

'Yes indeed. Because I know where this house in Spigonella is, but I don't know who it belongs to or if anyone's still living there. Have I made myself clear?'

'Crystal clear,' Mimì said sullenly.

'Ah, and one more thing. Get him to give you authorization to tap the phone line of one Gaetano Marzilla, who lives at Via Francesco Crispi 18, Montelusa. The sooner we listen in, the better.'

'What's Marzilla got to do with any of this?'

'Mimì, Marzilla's got nothing to do with this investigation. But he may be useful to me for something I have in mind. So I'll answer your question with a cliché that'll make you happy: I'm trying to kill two birds with one stone.'

'But—'

'Mimì, if you persist, I'm going to take the stone intended for those birds and—'

'OK, OK, I get the drift.'

✻

Fazio shuffled back to the office less than an hour later.

'It's all taken care of. Zito's going to broadcast the photo and the phone call on the two o'clock news. He sends regards.'

And he headed for the door.

'Wait.'

Fazio stopped, certain the inspector was going to say something else to him. But Montalbano said nothing. He only looked him up and down. Fazio, who knew him well, pulled up a chair. The inspector kept eyeing him. Fazio, however, was well aware that he wasn't really looking at him; he had his eyes on him, yes, but probably didn't see him because his mind was God-knows-where. And indeed, Montalbano was wondering whether he shouldn't perhaps ask Fazio to lend him a hand. But if he were to tell him the whole story of the African boy, how would Fazio react? Might he not reply that, in his opinion, this was all a figment of the inspector's imagination and had no basis in fact? On the other hand, by singing only half the Mass, Montalbano might be able to get some information without revealing too much.

'Listen, Fazio, do you know if there are any illegal immigrants working under the table in our area?'

Fazio didn't seem surprised by the question.

'There certainly are a lot of them everywhere, but right here, in our area, no.'

'Where are they, then?'

'Wherever there are greenhouses, vineyards, tomato

fields, orange groves ... Up north they work in industry, but around here, where there isn't any industry, they work in agriculture.'

The discussion was turning too general. Montalbano decided to narrow the field.

'What towns in our province would offer such possibilities for illegal workers?'

'To be honest, Chief, I couldn't really give you a complete list. Why are you interested?'

This was the question he feared most.

'Uh ... I was just wondering, that's all ...'

Fazio stood up, went to the door, closed it, and sat back down.

'Chief,' he said, 'would you be so kind as to tell me everything that's on your mind?'

Montalbano opened up, telling him every last thing, from the ill-fated evening on the wharf to his last meeting with Marzilla.

'There are quite a few greenhouses in Montechiaro,' said Fazio, 'with a hundred or so illegals working there. Maybe that's where the kid ran away from. The place where the car ran him down is only about three miles away.'

'Could you look into it?' the inspector ventured. 'But without telling anyone here at the station.'

'I can try,' said Fazio.

'You got something in mind?'

'Well ... I could try drawing up a list of people renting out houses – no, not houses, I mean stables, cellars, sewers!

— to illegals. They cram them in, ten at a time, in crawl spaces without windows! They do it under the table and charge them thousands. But maybe I could come up with something. Once I've got a list, I'll ask around if any of these illegals was recently joined by his wife ... It's not going to be easy, I can tell you straight away.'

'I know. I'm very grateful for your help.'

But Fazio didn't get up from his chair.

'What about tonight?' he asked.

The inspector immediately understood but assumed an angelic expression.

'What do you mean?' he said.

'Where's Marzilla going to pick up that guy at ten thirty?'

Montalbano told him.

'And what are you going to do?'

'Me? What am I supposed to do? Nothing.'

'Chief, you wouldn't be cooking up some brilliant scheme now, would you?'

'No, no, don't worry!'

'Bah!' said Fazio, getting up.

In front of the door, he stopped and turned around.

'Look, Chief, if you want, I'm free tonight and—'

'Jesus, what a pain! You're obsessed!'

'As if I didn't know you,' Fazio muttered, opening the door and going out.

*

'Turn on the television, quick!' he ordered Enzo as soon as he entered the trattoria.

The restaurateur looked at him in astonishment.

'What is this? Every time you come in and it's on, you want it turned off, and now that you find it off, you want it on?'

'You can turn the sound off,' Montalbano conceded.

Nicolò Zito kept his promise. At a certain point in the newscast (a collision between two caravans, a collapsed house, a man with his head split open for reasons that were unclear, a car on fire, a baby buggy overturned in the middle of the street, a woman tearing her hair out, a workman who fell from a scaffold, a man shot in a bar), the photo of Errera with the moustache appeared. Which meant all clear for Beba's little drama sketch. Meanwhile, all those images on the screen had the effect of spoiling his appetite. Before going back to the office, he went on a consolatory walk to the lighthouse.

＊

The door crashed, the plaster fell, Montalbano jumped, Catarella appeared. Ritual over.

'What the fuck! One of these days you're going to bring down the whole building!'

'I beck y' partin and fuggiveness, Chief, but when I'm ousside y' door, I git ixcited and my hand slips.'

'What makes you so excited?'

'Everyting 'bout you, Chief.'

'What do you want?'

'Pontius Pilate's 'ere.'

'Send him in. And hold all calls.'

'Even from the c'mishner?'

'Yes.'

'Even from Miss Livia?'

'Cat, I'm not here for anyone, can you get that through your head or do I have to do it for you?'

'Got it, Chief.'

FOURTEEN

Montalbano stood up to welcome the journalist and stopped halfway, dumbstruck. What appeared in the doorway had first looked to him like a gigantic walking bouquet of irises. In reality, it turned out to be a man of about fifty, dressed entirely in shades of blue-violet, a kind of round little pipsqueak, with round face, round belly, round eyes, round glasses, round smile. The only thing not round was his mouth; the lips were so big and red that they looked fake, as though painted. The man could certainly have had great success as a clown in a circus. He shot forward like a top and held his hand out to the inspector, who, in order to shake it, had to stretch forward lengthwise, belly resting on the desktop.

'Make yourself comfortable,' he said.

The bouquet of irises sat down. Montalbano couldn't believe his nostrils. The man even smelt like the flower. Cursing to himself, the inspector got ready to waste an hour of his time. Or maybe less. Surely he could think up some excuse to get rid of the guy. In fact, it was best to lay the groundwork immediately.

'I'm very sorry, Mr Pilate.'

'Spàlato.'

Blasted Catarella!

'... Mr Spàlato, you've caught me on an impossibly busy day. I've got very little time—'

The journalist raised a plump little hand, which to the inspector's surprise was not violet, but pink.

'I understand perfectly. I'll take up very little of your time. I wanted to begin with a question—'

'No, let me ask a question first: why and about what did you wish to talk to me?'

'Well, Inspector, a few nights ago I happened to be on the landing wharf at the port when two navy patrol boats were unloading some illegal immigrants and ... I caught sight of you there.'

'Oh, so that's why?'

'Yes. And I asked myself if there was any chance that a famous detective like you—'

The man was mistaken. The first mention of praise and flattery always put Montalbano on his guard. He closed up like a sea urchin and became a ball of thorns.

'Look, I was there entirely by chance. A question of spectacles.'

'Spectacles?' the other said in astonishment. But then he gave a sly little smile. 'I get it. You're trying to throw me off the trail!'

Montalbano stood up.

'I told you the truth and you didn't believe it. I think it would be a waste of my time and yours to proceed any further. Good day.'

The bouquet of irises stood up, looking suddenly wilted. With his little hand he shook the inspector's, which was held out to him.

'Good day,' he sighed, shuffling towards the door.

All of a sudden Montalbano felt sorry for him.

'Listen, if you're interested in the immigration problem, I can arrange for you to meet a colleague of mine who—'

'You mean Commissioner Riguccio? Thanks, but I've already spoken to him. He only sees the larger problem of illegal immigration and nothing else.'

'Why, is there some smaller problem we should be seeing inside a problem so large?'

'Yes, if one is willing to see it.'

'And what would that be?'

'The trafficking of immigrant children,' said Fonso Spàlato, opening the door and going out.

Exactly the way it happens in cartoons, two of the journalist's words – 'trafficking' and 'children' – material-ized in black, as though printed in mid-air, the rest of the room and everything in it having disappeared inside a kind of milky light, and after one millionth of a second the two words became intertwined, turning into two snakes that scuffled, fused, changed colour, then metamorphosed into a luminous globe from which a kind of lightning bolt shot forth and struck Montalbano between the eyes.

'Jesus Christ!' he cried out, grabbing hold of the desk.

In less than a second, all the scattered pieces of the puzzle swimming around in his head fell into place, fitting perfectly together. Then all went back to normal, and everything resumed its usual shape and colour. What did not return to normal was the inspector himself, because he couldn't move and his mouth stubbornly refused to open and call the journalist back. At last he managed to grab the telephone.

'Stop that journalist!' he shouted hoarsely at Catarella.

As he was sitting back down, wiping the sweat from his brow, he heard pandemonium break out on the street below. Somebody (it must have been Catarella) was yelling:

'Stop, Pontius Pilate!'

Somebody else (it must have been the journalist) said:

'What have I done? Let go of me!'

A third person (obviously some idiot passing by) took advantage of the situation to cry out:

'Down with the police!'

At last the door to the inspector's office flew open with a crash so loud that it visibly terrified the journalist who had just then appeared reluctantly in the doorway, pushed from behind by Catarella.

'Nabbed him, Chief!'

'What is going on? I don't understand—'

'My apologies, Mr Spàlato. An unfortunate misunder-standing. Please sit down.'

As Spàlato, more confused than convinced, came back in, the inspector brusquely commanded Catarella:

'Go away and shut the door!'

The iris bouquet collapsed in the chair, visibly withered. The inspector felt like spraying a little water on him to perk him up. But perhaps it was best to get right to the point that interested him, and make as though nothing had happened.

'You were talking about a certain traffic...'

Heri dicebamus. It worked like a charm. It didn't even occur to Spàlato to demand an explanation for the absurd treatment he had just been subjected to. In fresh bloom, he began.

'You know nothing about it, Inspector?'

'Nothing, I assure you. I would be very grateful if—'

'Just last year — these are the official figures — no less than fifteen thousand minors unaccompanied by an adult relation were tracked down in Italy.'

'Are you telling me they came over by themselves?'

'So it would seem. Of these minors, we can omit, at the very least, more than half.'

'Why?'

'Because in the meantime they've come of age. OK, nearly four thousand — a pretty high percentage, no? — came from Albania, the others from Romania, the former Yugoslavia and Moldavia. To this number we must add some thirteen hundred from Morocco, and more still from Algeria, Turkey, Iraq, Bangladesh and other countries. Getting a clear picture?'

'Quite. Their ages?'

'Right away.'

He took a small sheet of paper out of his jacket pocket, reviewed it, then put it back in his pocket.

'Two hundred aged nought to six; one thousand three hundred and sixteen between the ages of seven and fourteen; nine hundred and ninety-five aged fifteen; two thousand and eighteen aged sixteen; and three thousand nine hundred and twenty-four aged seventeen,' he recited. He looked at the inspector and sighed. 'But these are only the figures we know about. We also know that many hundreds of children disappear as soon as they enter the country.'

'What happens to them?'

'There are criminal organizations that have them specially brought here. These children are worth a fortune. They are also considered export commodities.'

'What for?'

Fonso Spàlato looked dumbfounded.

'You're asking me? Recently a member of Parliament from Trieste put together an enormous quantity of wiretap transcripts that talked about buying and selling immigrant children for organ recipients. The demand for transplants is huge and continually growing. Other minors are made available for paedophiles. Bear in mind that with that kind of child — alone, with no parents, relatives, nobody — there are people who will pay huge sums in order to practise certain kinds of extreme paedophilia.'

'Meaning?' asked Montalbano, his mouth dry.

'Involving torture and the violent death of the victim, to increase the pleasure of the paedophile.'

'I see.'

'Then there's the begging racket. The people who exploit little children by forcing them to beg for alms are very imaginative, you know. I once spoke with an Albanian boy who'd been kidnapped and then rescued by his father. His captors had crippled him, gravely injuring his knee and then purposely letting the wound fester, so passers-by would feel more sorry for him. Another kid got his hand cut off, and another—'

'Excuse me, I have to go out a minute. I just remembered something I need to do,' said the inspector, standing up.

As soon as he'd closed the door behind him, he bolted, racing past a befuddled Catarella like a hundred-metre sprinter, elbows chest-high, stride long and decisive. In the twinkling of an eye Montalbano arrived at the cafe on the corner, which at that moment was empty, and leaned against the bar.

'Gimme a triple whisky, neat.'

Without whispering a word, the barman served him. The inspector downed it in two gulps, paid, and left.

Catarella was planted firmly in front of the door to his office.

'What are you doing there?'

'I'm standin guard over the suspeck, Chief,' replied Catarella, gesturing towards the office with his head. 'Jessin case the suspeck tries to run away agin.'

'Good, you can go now.'

The inspector went in. The journalist hadn't moved from his place. Montalbano sat down at his desk. He felt better now, strong enough to listen to new horrors.

'I was asking you if these children leave their countries by themselves or if—'

'Inspector, I already told you there's a powerful criminal organization behind them. Some of them – a minority, actually – come over alone. Others are escorted.'

'By whom?'

'By people who pass themselves off as their parents.'

'Accomplices?'

'Well, I wouldn't be so explicit. You see, the journey is extremely expensive, and illegal immigrants make tremendous sacrifices to gain passage. But the price can be cut in half if they include a minor who's not part of the family with their own kids. But aside from these, so to speak, "chance" escorts, there are also the more usual escorts, who do it for the money. These are people who in every respect belong to this vast criminal organization. And they don't always bring the minor in by blending in with a group of illegal immigrants. There are other ways. Let me give you an example. One Friday a few months ago, a ship equipped for passenger and freight service from Durazzo puts in at the port of Ancona. An Albanian woman by the name of Giulietta Petalli, some thirty-odd years old, comes ashore. Attached to her standard residence permit is a photo of a child, her son, whom she is holding by the hand. By the time the lady arrives in Pescara, where she works, she's alone. The boy has disappeared. To make a long story short, the Pescara Flying Squad ascertained that sweet Giulietta, her husband, and an accomplice had together brought fifty-six different children into Italy. All vanished into thin air. What's wrong, Inspector, don't you feel well?'

A flash. For a moment, as a cramp wrenched his stomach, Montalbano saw himself taking the child by the hand, turning him over to the woman he thought was his mother ... And that look, those gaping eyes, which he would never be able to forget.

'Why?' he asked, feigning indifference.

'You look pale.'

'Every now and then it happens to me. It's a circulatory problem, nothing to worry about. But tell me something: if this odious traffic occurs in the Adriatic, why did you come here?'

'Simple. Because the slave-traders, for a variety of reasons, have been forced to change course. The one they've used for years is too well known. The screws have been tightened, and it's become much easier to intercept them. Bear in mind that last year alone, as I said, one thousand three hundred and fifty-eight minors came over from

Morocco. The already established sea-lanes in the Mediterranean had to be broadened and increased in number. And
this is what happened when the Tunisian, Baddar Gafsa,
became the unchallenged leader of the organization.'

'I'm sorry, I didn't get that. What was the name?'

'Baddar Gafsa, a character who, believe me, seems
straight out of a novel. Among other things, he goes by
the name of "Scarface", so you can imagine. He's a giant
who likes to load himself down with rings and bracelets
and always wears leather jackets. Barely thirty years old,
he has a veritable army of killers at his command, under
the leadership of his three lieutenants, Samir, Jamil, and
Ouled. He also has a fleet of trawlers, which are not, of
course, used for fishing, but are secretly moored in the inlets
at Capo Bono; these are under the command of Ghamun
and Ridha, two highly experienced sea captains who
know the Sicilian Channel as well as their bathroom sink.
Though the law's been after him for a long time, Gafsa
has never been caught. It is said that dozens of corpses
of enemies murdered by his own hand are hung on display
in his hideouts. He keeps them out for a while where
everyone can see them, to discourage potential traitors
but also to indulge his own sense of invincibility. Like
hunting trophies. You see, he travels a lot, going here and
there to settle, in his own special way, disputes among his
collaborators and to make examples of those who don't
obey his orders. And so his trophies keep growing in number.'

To Montalbano it seemed as if Spàlato were recounting the plot of a rather far-fetched adventure film of the kind the Italians used to call *americanate*.

'But how do you know these things? You seem very well informed to me.'

'Before coming to Vigàta I spent almost a month in Tunisia between Sfax and Sousse and all the way out to El Haduaria. I'd arranged beforehand to gain admission in the right places. And I'm experienced enough to know how to cut the fat of urban legends away from the truth.'

'You still haven't explained to me why you came specifically here, to Vigàta. Did you find something out in Tunisia that brought you here?'

Fonso Spàlato's vast mouth quadrupled in size as he smiled.

'You really are as intelligent as they say, Inspector. What I found out – and I won't tell you how, because it'd be too complicated, though I can vouch for the reliability of the source – is that Baddar Gafsa was seen in Lampedusa, on his way back from Vigàta.'

'When?'

'A little over two months ago.'

'And did they say what he was doing here?'

'They hinted at it. Anyway, it's important that you know that Gafsa has a huge sorting facility here.'

'In Vigàta?'

'Or nearby.'

'What do you mean by "sorting facility"?'

'A place where he has certain illegal aliens brought, the ones of great importance or value.'

'Such as?'

'Minors, as we were saying, or terrorists, or informers for infiltration, or persons already declared undesirable. He keeps them there before sending them out to their final destinations.'

'I see.'

'This sorting centre was in the hands of an Italian before Gafsa became head of the organization. Gafsa let him run things for a while, but then the Italian started getting ideas of his own. So Gafsa came over and killed him.'

'Do you know who he replaced him with?'

'Nobody, apparently.'

'So the "facility" is out of commission?'

'On the contrary. Let's just say there's no residing head, just local representatives who are informed, in due course, of imminent arrivals. When there's a big operation in the offing, then Jamil Zarzis, one of the three lieutenants, gets directly involved. He goes back and forth between Sicily and the Korba lagoon in Tunisia, where Gafsa has his headquarters.'

'You've given me a lot of Tunisian names, but not the name of the Italian murdered by Gafsa.'

'I don't know what his name was. I haven't been able to find out. I do know, however, what Gafsa's men called him. An utterly meaningless nickname.'

'What was it?'

'The dead man. That's what they called him, even when he was alive. Isn't that absurd?'

Absurd? Without warning, Montalbano stood up, threw his head back, and whinnied. It was a rather loud whinny, in every way like the noise a horse makes when it gets pissed off. Except that the inspector was not pissed off; quite the contrary. Everything had become clear. The parallel lines in the end had converged. Meanwhile the bouquet of irises, terrified, had slid off his chair and was heading for the door. Montalbano ran after him and grabbed him.

'Where are you going?'

'I'm going to call someone, you're obviously not well,' the irises stammered.

The inspector smiled broadly, to reassure him.

'No, please, it's nothing. These are just minor ailments, like my pallor a few minutes ago... I've been suffering from them for a long time. It's nothing serious.'

'Couldn't we perhaps open the door? I need some air.'

It was an excuse. Obviously the journalist wanted to keep a path of escape open.

'Sure, fine, we can open it.'

Mildly reassured, Fonso Spàlato went and sat back down. But he was clearly still nervous. He sat at the edge of the chair, ready to flee. He must have been wondering if he was indeed at Vigàta Police headquarters or in the province's remaining insane asylum. What disturbed him more than anything was the loving smile Montalbano beamed in his direction as he gazed at him. Indeed, at that moment the inspector was swept up in a wave of gratitude towards the man, who looked like a clown but was not. How could he ever repay him?

'Listen, Mr Spàlato. I haven't quite understood the reasons for your various travels. Did you come to Vigàta expressly to talk to me?'

'Yes. Unfortunately I have to go immediately back to Trieste. Mama is not well and she misses me. We're . . . very close.'

'Think you could stay another two days, three at the most?'

'Why?'

'Because I think I could get you, first-hand, some very important information.'

Fonso Spàlato thought about this a long time, his little eyes hidden behind closed lids. Then he decided to speak.

'At the start of our discussion, you told me you knew nothing about any of this.'

'It's true.'

'But if you didn't know anything, how can you say now that, in a very short space of time, you could get—'

'I didn't lie to you, believe me. You told me some things I didn't know before, but I now have the feeling those facts have put a current investigation of mine on the right track.'

'Well, I'm at the Regina in Montelusa. I think I could stay on another two days.'

'Excellent. Could you describe Gafsa's lieutenant, the one who often comes here? What's his name?'

'Jamil Zarzis. He's about forty, short and stocky... Or so at least I'm told... Oh, yes, one more thing: he has hardly any teeth.'

'Well, if, in the meantime, he's decided to see a dentist, we're screwed,' the inspector commented.

Fonso Spàlato threw his little hands in the air, as if to say that was all he knew about Jamil Zarzis.

'Listen, you told me Gafsa makes a point of eliminating his adversaries personally. Is that really true?'

'Yes.'

'A burst of Kalashnikov and goodnight, or—'

'No, he's a sadist. He's always finding new ways. I was told that he hung one man upside down until he died, and literally roasted another over hot coals; with yet another he bound his wrists and ankles with metal wire and slowly drowned him in the lagoon. Still another he—'

The inspector stood up. Worried, Fonso Spàlato fell silent.

'What's wrong?' he said, ready to jump out of his chair and start running.

'Do you mind if I whinny again?' the inspector politely asked.

FIFTEEN

'Who's that?' asked Mimì, watching Fonso Spàlato walk away down the corridor.

'An angel,' replied Montalbano.

'Right! In those clothes?'

'Why not? Do you think angels should only dress the way they do in the paintings of Melozzo da Forlì? Haven't you ever seen that Frank Capra movie called ... wait ...'

'Never mind,' said Mimì, who was obviously on edge. 'I wanted to tell you that Tommaseo phoned. I told him we'd be handling the case, but he wouldn't give us authorization to search the villa, nor would he consent to tapping Marzilla's phone. So the whole performance you orchestrated didn't help one goddamned bit.'

'That's OK, we'll work on our own. But could you explain why you're in such a bad mood?'

'You want to know why I'm in a bad mood?' Augello fired back at him. 'Because I listened to Beba's phone call to Tommaseo and I heard the kind of questions that pig asked her. I was standing there with my ear glued to the receiver. When she finished telling him what she'd seen, he started asking things like, "Were you alone in the car?" To which Beba replied with embarrassment, "No, I was with my boyfriend." So he said: "What were you doing?" And Beba, pretending to be even more embarrassed, "Well, you know..." So the pig says, "Were you making love?" Beba answers in a faint voice, "Yes..." And he asks, "Was the relation consummated?" Here Beba hesitated a moment, and so the swine explained to her that there were certain important facts he had to know in order to clarify the situation as much as possible. And at that point she stopped holding back and started getting into it. You have no idea the kinds of details she came out with! And the more she said, the more the pig got worked up! He actually wanted Beba to come in and testify in person! He wanted to know her name and what she looked like. To cut it short, after she hung up, we ended up quarrelling. My question is, where did she dig up some of those details?'

'Come on, Mimì, don't be childish! What, have you become jealous now?'

Mimì gave him a long look.

'Yes,' he said.

And he left the room.

'Send me Catarella!' the inspector shouted at him.

'Your orders, Chief!' said Catarella, instantly materializing.

'I think I remember you saying once that you often go visit a brother of yours who lives near Capo Russello.'

'Yessir, Chief.'

'Good. Can you explain to me how you get there?'

'No need to 'splain, Chief. I can come wit you myself in poisson!'

'Thanks, but this is something I have to take care of alone, no offence. So, can you explain to me how I get there?'

'Yessir. You take the road to Montereale and go past it. Keep goin for a coupla miles and on the left y'see an arrow that says Capo Russello.'

'Do I take that road?'

'No sir. You c'ntinue. Next you're gonna see an arrow that says Lampisa. That's the road you take.'

'OK, thanks.'

'Chief, that arrow that says Lampisa only says Lampisa in a manner o' speakin. Forget about goin to Lampisa if you only follow that arrow.'

'So what should I do?'

'When you take the road to Lampisa, you go about a hundred and fifty yards till you see a big iron gate that used to be there but isn't there no more.'

'How am I supposed to see a gate that isn't there?'

'Easy, Chief. 'Cause after where the gate used to be, there's two rows of oak trees. That used to be the Baron Vella's property, now it's nobody's property. When you come way to the back of that driveway an' you see the belapidated ruins of the baron's villa, you turn alla way around the last oak tree onna left. And not tree hunnert yards later you're in Lampisa.'

'And that's the only way to get there?'

'It depends.'

'Depends on what?'

'On if you're walkin or drivin there.'

'I'm driving.'

'Then iss the only way, Chief.'

'How far away is the sea?'

'Not a hunnert yards, Chief.'

*

To eat or not to eat? That was the question. Was it nobler in the mind to suffer the pangs of outrageous hunger or to hang it all and go and stuff his belly at Enzo's? The Shakespearian dilemma arose when he looked at his watch and noticed it was already eight o'clock. If he gave in to hunger, that would give him just barely an hour to devote to dinner. Which meant that he would have to eat with Chaplinesque speed. Now, one thing was certain, and that was that eating hastily was not eating. At best it was mere self-nourishment. An essential difference, since at that moment he felt no need to nourish himself the way an animal or a tree might. What he felt like doing was savouring bite after bite, taking as much time as was needed. No, there was no point. And, to avoid falling into temptation, once he got home he opened neither the refrigerator nor the oven. He took all his clothes off and went into the shower. Then he put on a pair of jeans and a Canadian bear-hunter's shirt. It occurred to him that he didn't know how things would go, and he wondered: to pack or not to pack? Perhaps it was better to bring his pistol. Then he picked out a dark brown jacket that had a spacious inner pocket and put this on. He didn't want to alarm Ingrid if at some point he needed to fetch his weapon; better get it now. He went outside to the car, opened the glove compartment, grabbed the pistol, and slipped it in the inside pocket of the jacket. When he bent down to close the glove compartment, the gun slid out of the pocket and fell to the floor of the car. Montalbano cursed the saints, got down on his knees – because the gun had ended up under the seat – picked it up, locked the car, and went back in the house. Feeling hot with his jacket on, he took it off and set it down on the dining-room table. He decided it was a good time to call Livia. He picked up the receiver, dialled the number, and just as the first ring began, the doorbell rang as well. To open or not to open? He hung up and went to open the door. It was Ingrid, a little early. More beautiful than ever, if that was possible. To kiss her or not to kiss her? The question was answered at once by the Swede, who kissed him.

'How are you?'

'I feel a little like Hamlet.'

'I don't understand.'

'Never mind. Did you come in your husband's car?'

'Yes.'

'What is it?'

An utterly academic question. Montalbano didn't know a bloody thing about cars. Or motors, for that matter.

'A BMW 320.'

'What colour?'

This question, on the other hand, had a specific purpose. Knowing what an idiot Ingrid's husband was, he was likely to have had it painted in red, yellow, and green stripes with blue polka dots.

'Dark grey.'

Thank heavens. There was a chance they might not be spotted and shot right off the bat.

'Have you had dinner?' asked Ingrid.

'No. How about you?'

'No, I haven't either. Later, if there's time, we could . . . By the way, what are we doing tonight?'

'I'll explain on the way there.'

The telephone rang. It was Marzilla.

'Inspector, the car they brought me is a Jaguar. I'll be leaving my place in five minutes,' he said in a quavering voice.

Then he hung up.

'If you're ready, we can go now,' said Montalbano.

He put on his jacket with nonchalance, not realizing it

was inside out. Naturally the gun slid out of the pocket and fell to the floor. Ingrid recoiled in fright.

'Are you serious?' she asked.

*

Following Catarella's instructions, they didn't miss a single turn. Half an hour after they'd left Marinella – half an hour which Montalbano used to fill Ingrid in – they arrived at the lane of oaks. They took this, and when they'd reached the end, they saw, by the light of the headlights, the ruins of a large villa.

'Go straight,' said Montalbano. 'Don't follow the road and don't turn left. We have to hide the car behind the villa.'

Ingrid did as he said. Behind the villa was open, desolate country. She turned off the headlights and they got out. The moon lit their way. The night was so quiet, it was frightening. They didn't even hear any dogs barking.

'What now?' asked Ingrid.

'We leave the car here and we go and find a place from where we can see the lane, so we can watch the cars that go by.'

'What cars?' said Ingrid. 'Here we won't even see any crickets go by.'

They headed off.

'Well, we can do what they do in movies,' said Ingrid again.

'Why, what do they do in movies?'

'Come on, Salvo, don't you know? When the two police officers, a man and a woman, stake out a place, they pretend they're lovers. They embrace and kiss, but they're actually keeping watch.'

Now they were right in front of the villa, about thirty yards from the oak tree where the road turned towards Lampisa. They sat down on the remains of a wall and Montalbano lit a cigarette. But he didn't have time to finish it. A car had come down the lane, advancing slowly. Perhaps the driver didn't know the road. Ingrid leapt to her feet, held her hand out to the inspector, pulled him to his feet, and wrapped her arms around him. The car approached very slowly. For Montalbano it was like being wholly enveloped by the branches of an apricot tree. The scent made his head spin, stirring up what there was to stir up in him. Ingrid held him very tightly. At one point she whispered in his ear:

'Something's moving.'

'Where?' asked Montalbano, chin resting on her shoulder, nose drowning in her hair.

'Between us, down below,' said Ingrid.

Montalbano felt himself blush and tried to pull his hips back, but Ingrid kept him plastered against her.

'Don't be silly,' she said.

For a second the car's headlights shone directly on them, then it turned left at the last oak tree and disappeared.

'That was your car, a Jaguar,' said Ingrid.

Montalbano thanked the Good Lord that Marzilla had arrived in time. He couldn't have held out another minute. Breathing heavily, he pulled away from Ingrid.

*

It wasn't a chase because at no point did Marzilla or the other two men in the Jaguar have the feeling that another car was following them. Ingrid was an exceptional driver. For as long as they were off the main road to Vigàta, she drove without headlights, guided only by the moonlight. She didn't turn them on until they reached the main road, since she could easily hide in the traffic. Marzilla drove along briskly, though not overly fast, and this made it easier to shadow him. It was like following someone on foot. Marzilla's Jaguar turned onto the road for Montelusa.

'I feel like I'm out for a boring Sunday drive,' said Ingrid.

Montalbano didn't answer.

'Why did you bring your gun?' she continued. 'You haven't been needing it much.'

'Disappointed?'

'Yes, I was hoping for something more exciting.'

'Well, never fear. We're not in the clear yet, something could still happen.'

After Montelusa, the Jaguar took the road for Montechiaro.

Ingrid yawned.

'Ouf! I have half a mind to let them know we're following them.'

'Why?'

'To shake things up a little.'

'Don't do anything stupid!'

The Jaguar drove past Montechiaro and took the road that led to the coast.

'You drive for a while,' said Ingrid. 'I'm bored.'

'No.'

'Why not?'

'First of all, because soon there won't be any more cars on the road and you'll have to turn off the headlights to avoid being spotted. And I can't drive by moonlight.'

'And second?'

'And second, because you know this road a lot better than I do, especially at night.'

Ingrid turned a moment to face him.

'You know where they're going?'

'Yes.'

'Where?'

'To the villa of your former friend Ninì D'Iunio, as he used to call himself.'

The BMW swerved, almost ending up in a field, but Ingrid quickly got it under control. She said nothing. When they got to Spigonella, instead of taking the road the inspector knew, Ingrid turned right.

'That's not the—'

'I know,' said Ingrid, 'but we can't keep following the Jaguar here. There's only one road that goes to the promontory and the house. They would definitely see us.'

'And so?'

'So I'm taking us to a spot from where we can see the front of the house. And we'll get there a little before they do.'

Ingrid stopped the BMW at the edge of a cliff, behind a Moorish-style bungalow.

'Let's get out. They can't see our car from here, but we'll have an excellent view of them.'

They went around the bungalow. On their left they had a clear view of the promontory and the road leading to the villa. Less than a minute later, the Jaguar pulled up to the closed gate. They heard two very brief toots of the horn, followed by a long one. Then the door on the ground floor opened, and against the light they saw the silhouette of a man going to open the gate. The Jaguar drove in, and the man walked back to the house, leaving the gate open.

'Let's go,' said Montalbano. 'There's nothing more to see here.'

They got back in the car.

'Now, turn on the engine,' said the inspector, 'and, with headlights off, we're going to go to ... Do you remember that small red-and-white villa where Spigonella begins?'

'Yes.'

'Good. We're going to take up position there. To go back to Montechiaro, one has to drive by that spot.'

'Who has to drive by that spot?'

'The Jaguar.'

Ingrid barely had time to get to the red-and-white house before the Jaguar went flying by at high speed, skidding at the curve.

Apparently Marzilla wanted to put as much distance as possible between him and the men he'd driven to the villa.

'What should I do?' asked Ingrid.

'Now shalt thou prove thy mettle,' said Montalbano.

'I didn't get that. What did you say?'

'Follow him. Use your horn, your brights, get up right behind him, pretend you're going to ram him. You have to terrorize the man at the wheel.'

'Leave it to me,' said Ingrid.

For a stretch she drove on without headlights and at a safe distance; then, when the Jaguar disappeared behind a bend, she accelerated, turned on all available and imaginable headlights, rounded the bend and started wildly honking the horn.

Seeing that unexpected missile come up behind him must have frightened Marzilla out of his wits.

First the Jaguar zigzagged, then it veered all the way to the right and off the road, thinking the other car wanted to pass it. But Ingrid did not pass him. Riding right on the Jaguar's tail, she was flashing the brights on and off and continually blasting the horn. Desperate, Marzilla accelerated, but he couldn't go much faster on that road. Ingrid didn't let up; her BMW was like a mad dog.

'What now?'

'When you get a chance, pass him, make a U-turn in front of him, and stop in the middle of the road with your brights on.'

'I could even do it right now. Put on your seat belt.'

The BMW leapt forward, roared, passed the other car, drove on a bit, braked, skidded, then spun around on the force of the skid. The Jaguar, too, came to a skidding stop just a few yards away, in the glare of the BMW's high beam. Montalbano pulled out his pistol, stuck his arm outside the window, and fired a shot in the air.

'Turn off your headlights and come out with your hands up!' he shouted through the half-open car door.

The Jaguar's lights went off and Marzilla appeared with his hands in the air. Montalbano didn't move. Marzilla was swaying like a tree in the wind.

'He's pissing his trousers,' Ingrid commented.

Montalbano remained motionless. Slowly, two big tears started to run down the medical worker's face. He took a step forward, dragging his feet.

'Have pity!'

Montalbano didn't answer.

'Have pity, Don Pepè! What do you want from me? I did what you wanted!'

Montalbano still wasn't moving. Marzilla fell to his knees, hands folded in prayer.

'Please don't kill me! Please don't kill me, Mr Aguglia!'

So the loan shark who was calling Marzilla and giving

him orders was Don Pepè Aguglia, a well-known construction bigwig. They hadn't needed any wiretaps to find out.
Marzilla was now crouching, forehead on the ground,
hands over his head. Montalbano finally decided to get out
of the car. Which he did very slowly. Hearing his footsteps
approach, Marzilla curled up even more, sobbing.

'Look at me, arsehole.'

'No, no!'

'Look at me!' Montalbano repeated, kicking him so
hard in the ribs that Marzilla's body was lifted up in the
air and fell back down belly up. But he still kept his eyes
desperately closed.

'It's Montalbano! Look at me!'

It took Marzilla a moment to realize that the man
standing before him was not Don Pepè Aguglia, but the
inspector. He sat up, leaning back on one arm. He must
have bitten his tongue, since a little blood trickled out the
side of his mouth. He stank. He hadn't only pissed his
trousers, he'd also shat himself.

'Oh ... it's you? Why did you follow me?' asked
Marzilla, stunned.

'Me?' said Montalbano, innocent as a lamb. 'It was a
mistake. I wanted you to stop, and you started going faster!
So I thought you had wicked intentions.'

'What ... what do you want from me?'

'Tell me what language the two men you drove to the
villa were speaking.'

'Arabic, I think.'

'Who told you which roads to take and where you were supposed to go?'

'Just one of the men.'

'Did it seem to you like he'd been here before?'

'Yessir.'

'Could you describe them to me?'

'Only one of them, the guy who spoke. He didn't have any teeth.'

Jamil Zarzis, Gafsa's lieutenant, had arrived.

'Do you have a mobile phone?'

'Yes. It's on the front seat of the car.'

'Did anyone call you, or did you call anyone after you dropped the two men off?'

'No sir.'

Montalbano went up to the Jaguar, grabbed the mobile phone, and put it in his pocket. Marzilla didn't breathe.

'Now get back in the car and go home.'

Marzilla tried to stand up, but couldn't.

'Let me give you a hand,' said the inspector.

He grabbed him by the hair and jerked him to his feet as the man cried out in pain. Then with a violent kick in the back he sent him reeling into the front seat of the Jaguar. Marzilla took a good five minutes to leave, so badly were his hands shaking. Montalbano waited until the red tail-lights disappeared before going back to Ingrid's car and sitting beside her.

'I didn't know you were ... capable of ...' Ingrid muttered.

'Of what?'

'I don't know how to put it. Of ... being so nasty.'

'Me neither,' said Montalbano.

'What did the guy do?'

'He did ... he gave an injection to a little boy who didn't want one,' was the best he could come up with.

Ingrid looked completely perplexed.

'So you take revenge on him because you were afraid of getting injections when you were a child?'

Psychoanalyse though she might, Ingrid couldn't know that in manhandling Marzilla, he had really wanted to manhandle himself.

'Come on, let's go,' said the inspector. 'Take me home. I'm tired.'

SIXTEEN

It was a lie. He did not feel tired. In fact he felt eager to get down to work. But he had to get rid of Ingrid as soon as possible. He didn't have a minute to lose. He managed to dispatch her without betraying his haste, thanking her and kissing her and promising they'd meet again the following Saturday. Once he was alone at home in Marinella, the inspector turned into one of those high-speed heroes in old slapstick movies, shooting like a rocket from room to room in a desperate search. Where the hell had he put that wetsuit after he'd last used it to look for the *ragioniere* Gargano's car at the bottom of the sea a good two years back? He turned the house upside down and finally found it in an inner drawer of the armoire, properly wrapped in plastic. But what really drove him crazy was that he couldn't find a pistol holster that he practically never used but which nevertheless had to be somewhere. In fact, it turned out to be in the bathroom, inside the shoe rack, under a pair of slippers he had never dreamed of wearing. Hiding it there must have been a brilliant idea of Adelina's. The house now looked like it had been ransacked by a bunch of wine-plastered landsknechts. He had probably best not cross paths in the morning with his housekeeper, who would be in a bad mood when she saw how much work he had made for her.

He undressed, put on the wetsuit, passed the belt through the holster's loop, then put only his jeans and jacket back on. Passing in front of a mirror, he caught a glimpse of himself. First he felt like laughing, then he felt embarrassed. He looked dressed up for a movie. What was this, Carnival or something?

'The name's Bond. James Bond,' he said to his reflection.

He consoled himself with the thought that at this hour he wouldn't run into anyone he knew. He put the espresso pot on the burner, and when the coffee was ready, he knocked back three cups in a row. Before going out, he looked at his watch. At a rough guess, he would be back in Spigonella by two o'clock in the morning.

✻

He was so lucid and determined that on his very first try he found the road Ingrid had taken, which led to the spot from where one could see the front of the villa. The last hundred yards he had to drive without headlights. His only fear was that he might drive the car straight into the damn sea. He pulled up behind the Moorish-style bungalow perched at the edge of the cliff, turned off the engine, grabbed his binoculars, and got out. He leaned forward to look. There was no light visible in the windows. The villa looked uninhabited, and yet there were three men inside. Very carefully, dragging his feet the way people do when they can't see very well, he advanced to the edge of the cliff and looked below. He couldn't see anything, but he could hear the sea, which sounded a little rough. With the binoculars he tried to see if there was any activity in the villa's little harbour, but he could barely make out the darker shapes of the rocks.

To the right, about ten yards away, was a narrow, steep staircase, carved into the stone wall. Negotiating it would have been a task for an alpinist in broad daylight, let alone in the dead of night. But he had no choice; there was no other way to get down to the beach. He went back beside the car, slipped off his jeans and jacket, took out his pistol, opened the car door, threw his stuff inside, grabbed his underwater torch, took the keys from the glove compartment, closed the car door without a sound, and hid the keys by wedging them under the right rear tyre. He fitted the gun into the holster on his belt, slung the binoculars across his chest, and kept the torch in his hand. On the very first step, he stopped, trying to get a sense of the stairway's configuration. He turned the torch on for a second and looked. He felt himself begin to sweat inside the wetsuit: the steps went down almost vertically.

✻

Flicking the torch very quickly on and off from time to time to see whether his foot would land on solid ground or merely plunge into the void, and meanwhile cursing, hesitating, staggering, slipping, grabbing on to roots sticking out from the rock face, regretting that he wasn't an ibex, deer, or even a lizard, he finally, when the Good Lord saw fit, felt cool sand under the soles of his feet. He'd made it.

He lay down on his back, panting heavily, and watched the stars. He stayed that way for a while, until the bellows in the place of his lungs slowly disappeared. He stood up and looked through the binoculars. The dark shapes of the rocks that broke up the beach and formed the villa's little harbour looked to be about fifty yards away. He started walking, crouching down and hugging the rock face. Every few steps he would stop, ears pricked, eyes as wide open as possible. Nothing. Total silence. All was still except the sea.

When he was almost behind the rocks, he looked up. All he could see of the villa was a kind of rectangular railing against the starry sky – in other words, the underside of the vast terrace balcony at the point where it jutted out most. From here he couldn't advance any further by land. He put the binoculars down on the sand, hooked the underwater torch onto his belt, took another step, and was in the water. He didn't expect it to be as deep as it was, coming immediately up to his chest. He figured this couldn't be a natural phenomenon; they must have dug into the sand to create a sort of moat, to add another obstacle for anyone on the beach who felt like climbing the rocks.

He started swimming slowly, using a breaststroke, girl-style, to avoid even the slightest splashing, following the curve of that arm of the little harbour. The water was cold, and as he drew near the opening, the waves grew increasingly strong, threatening to send him scraping against some jagged rock. As there was now no longer any need to do the breaststroke – since any noise he might make would blend in with the sound of the sea – in four rapid crawl strokes he reached the last rock, the one marking the opening. He was leaning against it with his left hand, to catch his breath a moment, when a wave more powerful than the rest pushed him forward, knocking his feet against a very small natural platform. He climbed up on it, clinging to the rock with both hands. With each new wave he risked slipping, pulled down by the undertow. It was a dangerous spot, but before proceeding he had to get a few things straight.

According to his memory of the video, the other rock marking the entranceway should have been further in, closer to shore, since the second arm of the little harbour described a large question mark, the upper curl of which ended with that very rock. Sticking his head out sideways, he saw its shadow. He paused a moment to look; he wanted to make certain there was nobody keeping guard on the other side. When he was sure of this, he inched his feet ever so slowly to the edge of the natural platform, then again had to assume a precarious posture, standing and fully stretching out vertically so that his hand could blindly feel about for something metal, the small signal light he'd managed to make out in the photographic enlargement. It took him a good five minutes to find it. It was higher up than it had looked to him in the photo. As a precaution, he ran his hand over it several times. He heard no alarm go off in the distance. So it wasn't an electric eye, but indeed a beacon turned off at that moment. He waited yet another minute for some sort of reaction, but when nothing at all happened, he dived back into the water. Halfway around the rock, his hand suddenly ran into the metal barrier preventing any surprise visits to the little harbour. Still groping, he ascertained that the barrier slid along a vertical rail that must be electronically controlled from inside the villa.

All that was left to do now was to go inside. He grabbed onto the barrier so he could hoist himself up and climb over it. He'd already got his left foot over when it happened. What 'it' was, Montalbano couldn't quite say. The pain in the middle of his chest was so sudden, so sharp, and so unceasing that the inspector, collapsing while straddling the barrier, was convinced someone had shot him with an underwater rifle and made a direct hit. But at the same time he was thinking this, it became clear to him that he was wrong. He bit his lips to suppress the desperate wail he so wanted to let out, which might have provided some relief. Then he realized at once that the stabbing pain did not come from the outside, as he already obscurely knew, but from the inside — from inside his body, where something had broken or was at the breaking point. It became very difficult to take a breath of air through his closed lips. Then suddenly, as quickly as it had appeared, the pain stopped, leaving him aching and numb, but not scared. Surprise had got the better of fear. He slid his buttocks along the top of the barrier until he could lean his shoulders against the rock. His sense of balance was no longer so precarious. He still had a chance and some time to recover from the malaise that the terrible bout of pain had left behind. But no, he had no chance and no time at all, as a second stab shot through his chest implacably, more ferocious than the first. He tried to control himself but couldn't. He hunched forward and started crying, eyes closed, weeping from pain and dejection, unable to distinguish the taste of his tears when they reached his mouth from the droplets of seawater trickling down from his hair. As the pain became a kind of hot drill boring into his flesh, he chanted to himself:

'O Father, my father, my father...'

He was praying to his dead father and wordlessly asking him to intercede and make someone finally spot him from the villa's terrace and finish him off with a compassionate burst of machine-gun fire. But his father didn't hear the prayer, and Montalbano kept on crying until, once again, the pain disappeared, though very slowly this time, as though it regretted leaving his body.

A long time passed before he was in any condition to move a hand or a foot. It was as though his limbs refused to obey his brain's commands. Were his eyes open or closed? Was it darker than before, or had his sight grown dim?

He resigned himself. He had to accept things as they were. He'd been stupid to come alone. Something had gone wrong, and now he had to pay the price for his bravado. All he could do was take advantage of the lulls between attacks to slip back in the water and swim slowly around the rock and towards the shore. There was no point in proceeding any further. He had to go back. He needed only to get back in the water, swim just around the buoy, and . . .

Why had he thought 'buoy' instead of 'rock'? Then the scene he'd viewed on television came back to him – the proud refusal of that yacht which, instead of rounding the mark and turning back, had stubbornly careered forward, finally crashing into the referees' boat – and he realized that, being the way he was, he had no choice. He could never turn back.

He stayed there, motionless, for half an hour, leaning against the rock, listening to his body, waiting for the slightest sign of a new attack. Nothing else happened. But he couldn't let any more time go by. He slipped back into the sea on the inside of the barrier and began swimming with a breaststroke, since the water was calm and the waves weak, having already broken against the barrier. Making for the shore, he realized he was inside a kind of canal at least twenty feet wide with cement banks. And while he still could not touch the bottom, on his right he saw a whiteness of sand, at the level of his head. Placing his hands on the bank, he hoisted himself up.

Looking ahead, he was astonished to find that the canal did not end at the beach, but cut it in two and continued into a natural grotto completely invisible to anyone passing by in front of the little harbour or looking out from the cliff overhead. A grotto! A few yards from the entrance, on the right, was another staircase carved into the rock, similar to the one he'd come down, except that this one was blocked by a gate. Crouching down, he went up to the mouth of the cave and listened. No sound at all, other than the lapping of the water inside. He flopped belly-down on the ground, unhooked the torch, flicked it on for a second, then turned it off. He stored in his brain everything the flash of light had allowed him to see, then repeated the procedure, taking in a few more precious details. After the third flash, he knew what was inside the grotto.

Rocking in the middle of the canal was a large dinghy, probably a Zodiac, which came with a powerful motor. Along the right-hand side of the canal was a cement quay just over a yard wide. Halfway down this quay there was a huge iron door, which was shut. It probably led to a hangar where the dinghy was kept when not in use, and even more likely to an internal staircase that went up to the villa. Or a lift. There was no telling. It was also clear that the grotto went even further back, but the dinghy blocked his view of what lay behind it.

What now? Should he stop here? Keep going?

'Here goes nothing,' Montalbano said to himself.

He stood up and entered the grotto without lighting his torch. Feeling the cement of the wharf under his feet, he slowly advanced. His right hand grazed the rusty iron door. He brought his ear to it. Nothing. Total silence. He put his hand on it and felt it give. It was barely pulled to. He pressed lightly, and this sufficed to open it about an inch. The hinges must have been well oiled. But what if someone had heard him and was waiting for him with a Kalashnikov? Too bad. He grabbed his pistol and switched on the torch. Nobody fired, nobody even said hello. He was inside the dinghy's hangar. It was full of jerry cans. At the back there was an arch carved into the rock and, beyond this, some steps. The staircase leading up to the villa, as he'd imagined. He turned off the torch and closed the door behind him. He took another three steps, then gave himself some light. The quay went on for another few yards then suddenly ended, giving way to a kind of lookout at the back of the grotto, a great accumulation of rocks of various sizes piled high, a kind of chaotic, miniature mountain chain under the soaring vault overhead. He turned off the light.

But what was it about those rocks? There was something strange there. As he tried to understand why the rocks looked strange to him, Montalbano, in the darkness and silence, heard a sound that made his blood run cold. There was something alive in the grotto. It made a continuous scraping noise, staggered by a kind of ticking, like wood against wood. He noticed that the air he was breathing had a rotten yellow colour about it. Alarmed, he turned the torch on and off again. It was enough to let him see that the rocks, green with sea-moss at the water level, changed colour above, because they were literally covered by hundreds, indeed thousands, of crabs of every size and colour, continuously moving, swarming, climbing over one another until they formed great living horrendous clusters that came apart under their own weight and fell into the water. A disgusting spectacle.

Montalbano also noticed that the back of the grotto was separated from the front by a wire fence that rose about a foot and a half above the water and ran from the edge of the wharf to the rock face opposite. What could that be for? To keep big fish from coming in? What the hell was he thinking? Perhaps, on the contrary, it was to keep something from going out? But what, if there was nothing in the grotto but rocks and crabs?

All at once he understood. What had Dr Pasquano said? That the corpse had been eaten up by crabs, and he'd even found two in its throat... This was where Errera–D'Iunio, who'd got a bit too headstrong, was punished by drowning. Baddar Gafsa then let the body steep a long time in the water, right here, wrists and ankles bound with metal wire, as the crabs ate it up, another trophy to show to friends and anyone who might feel tempted to betray him. Finally he had it dumped into the open sea. And sailing, sailing, the body ended up off the shore at Marinella.

What else was there to see? He retraced his steps, went out of the grotto, got in the water, swam, climbed over the barrier, swam around the rock, and felt suddenly overwhelmed by a deadly, endless fatigue. And this time he felt scared. He hadn't even the strength to raise his arm to keep swimming. He'd suddenly run out of steam. Apparently the only thing that had kept him going was nervous tension, and now that he'd done what he had to do, there was nothing left in his body to give him even a little jolt. He turned over onto his back and began to float. It was all he could do. Sooner or later the tide would carry him ashore. At some point he seemed to wake up, when he felt his back scrape against something. Had he nodded off? Was it possible? In that sea, and in those conditions, had he fallen asleep as in a bathtub? Whatever the case, he realized he'd reached a beach, but he couldn't stand up. His legs wouldn't support him. He lay down on his belly and looked around. The current had taken pity on him and carried him back very near the spot where he'd set down the binoculars. He couldn't very well leave them there. But how to get to that spot? After trying two or three times to stand, he resigned himself to crawling on all fours like an animal. Every yard or so he had to stop, out of breath and sweating. When he was next to the binoculars, he couldn't grab them. His arm wouldn't reach out; it refused to solidify; it was like a mass of quivering jelly. He gave up. He would have to wait. But he didn't have much time to waste. At daybreak the people in the villa would see him.

'Just five minutes,' he said to himself, closing his eyes and curling up on his side like a child.

He needed only to put a finger in his mouth to complete the picture. For the moment he wanted to sleep a little, to recover his strength. In any case, in his current state, he could never manage to climb that terrible staircase. But no sooner had he closed his eyes than he heard a noise very near, and a violent light shone straight through his eyelids, as if they'd disappeared.

They'd found him! He knew it was the end. But he was so drained of strength, so happy just to keep his eyes closed, that he didn't react and didn't move from his position, utterly indifferent to what was about to happen to him.

'Just shoot me and go fuck yourself,' he said.

'And why would you want me to shoot you?' asked Fazio in a strangled voice.

*

Going up the stairway, he had to stop after almost every step, even though Fazio had a hand on his back and was pushing him from behind. They had only five stairs to go when he needed to sit down. His heart was up in his windpipe, and he felt that at any moment it might leap right out of his mouth. Fazio also sat down, in silence. Montalbano couldn't see his face, but felt his agitation and anger.

'How long have you been following me?'

'Since yesterday evening. After Miss Ingrid dropped you off at home, I didn't leave right away. I decided to wait a bit. I had a feeling you might go out again. Which you did. I managed to follow you easily up to Spigonella, then I lost you. You'd think I ought to know the area by now. It took me almost an hour to find your car.'

Montalbano looked down. The sea had swelled with the rising wind, which already smelt of the imminent dawn. If not for Fazio, he would surely still be down on the beach, half conscious. It was Fazio who had picked up the damned binoculars, put him on his feet, practically carried him on his shoulders, and forced him to react. He had, in other words, saved him. He took a deep breath.

'Thanks.'

Fazio didn't answer.

'But you never came here with me,' the inspector continued.

Again Fazio said nothing.

'Will you give me your word?'

'Yes. But will you give me yours?'

'What for?'

'Promise me you'll go see a doctor. As soon as possible.'

Montalbano swallowed this bitter pill.

'Promise,' he said, getting up.

He was convinced he would keep his word. Not because he feared for his health, but because one cannot break a promise made to one's guardian angel. And he resumed the climb.

✳

He had no problem driving along the still-deserted streets, dogged by Fazio's car behind him. There'd been no convincing his sergeant that he could easily make it home by himself. Slowly, as the sky began to brighten, the inspector began to feel better. The day looked promising. They went into his house.

'Jesus Christ! You've been robbed!' yelled Fazio as soon as he saw the state the rooms were in.

'No, it was me. I was looking for something.'

'Did you find it?'

'Yes.'

'It's a good thing you did, or you would have torn down the walls!'

'Listen, Fazio, it's almost five. I'll see you at the office sometime after ten, OK?'

'OK, Chief. Get some rest.'

'And I want to see Inspector Augello, too.'

*

After Fazio left, the inspector wrote a note to Adelina, in block letters:

> *ADELINA, DON'T BE ALARMED.*
> *THE HOUSE HAS NOT BEEN BURGLED.*
> *PLEASE TIDY UP BUT DON'T MAKE*
> *ANY NOISE BECAUSE I'M SLEEPING.*
> *PLEASE MAKE ME SOMETHING TO EAT.*

He opened the front door and stuck the note to it with a drawing-pin, so the housekeeper would see it before she came in. He unplugged the phone, went in the bathroom, took a shower, dried himself off, and lay down on the bed. The terrible bout of weakness had miraculously passed. In truth, he felt a bit tired, but no more than usual, and it had, after all, been a rough night, there was no denying it. He ran a hand over his chest, as if to check if the two terrible pangs had left some kind of mark, some kind of scar. Nothing. No wound opened, no wound healed. Before falling asleep, he had one last thought, with all due respect to his guardian angel: was it really so necessary to see a doctor? No, he concluded. He really saw no need for it.

SEVENTEEN

He arrived at the office at eleven, all slicked up and, if not
smiling, at least not in a bearish mood. The hours of sleep
had actually rejuvenated him. He could feel all the gears
in his body working at maximum efficiency. Of the two
terrible chest pains of the night before and the weakness
that had followed, not a trace. In the doorway he nearly
bumped into Fazio, who was coming out, and who, upon
seeing him, stopped short and eyed him up and down. The
inspector let him eye.

'You look good this morning,' was the verdict.

'I changed foundation cream,' said Montalbano.

'No, the truth of the matter is that you, Chief, have
nine lives, like a cat. I'll be right back.'

The inspector went and stood in front of Catarella.

'How do I look to you?'

'Whattya want me to say, Chief? Like a god!'

When you came right down to it, this much-maligned
cult of personality wasn't really such a bad thing.

Mimì Augello also looked well rested.

'Did Beba let you sleep last night?'

'Yes, we had a good night. In fact, she didn't want me to come to work today.'

'Why not?'

'She wanted me to take her out, since it's such a beautiful day. Poor thing, lately she never leaves the house anymore.'

'Here I am,' said Fazio.

'Close the door and we can begin.'

*

'I'm going to give a general summary,' Montalbano began, 'even though you already know some of the details. If there's anything that doesn't make sense to you, let me know.'

He spoke for half an hour without interruption, explaining how Ingrid had recognized D'Iunio and how his parallel investigation into the African boy had slowly converged with the investigation of the nameless drowned man. Then he described what Fonso Spàlato had told him in turn. When he came to the point where Marzilla got scared shitless after dropping off Jamil Zarzis and another man at the villa, he interrupted himself and asked:

'Are there any questions?'

'Yes,' said Augello, 'but first I must ask Fazio to leave the room, count slowly to ten, then come back inside.'

Without a peep, Fazio got up, went out, and closed the door.

'The question is this,' said Augello, 'when are you going to stop acting like an arsehole?'

'In what sense?'

'In every sense, for Christ's sake! Who do you think you are, the night avenger? The lone wolf? You're a fucking police inspector! Have you forgotten? You reproach the police for not obeying the rules, and you're the first to break them! You go out on a dangerous mission, and you bring along not one of us, but a Swedish lady! It's insane! You should have informed your superiors of all these things, or at least filled us in, instead of going out and playing the bounty hunter!'

'So that's what's bugging you?'

'Why, isn't that enough?'

'No, it's not, Mimì. I've done worse.'

Mimì's jaw dropped in horror.

'Worse?'

'And ten,' said Fazio, reappearing.

'To continue,' said Montalbano. 'When Ingrid cut in front of Marzilla's car, he thought we were his boss and were going to liquidate him, perhaps because at this point he knows too much. He pissed his trousers as he begged me not to kill him. And without even realizing it, he blurted out his boss's name: Don Pepè Aguglia.'

'The builder?' asked Augello.

'That's him, all right,' Fazio confirmed. 'There are rumours around town that he's been loan-sharking.'

'We'll take care of him very soon — tomorrow, in fact

— but somebody should keep an eye on him starting now. I don't want him to slip away.'

'Leave him to me,' said Fazio. 'I'll put Curreli on his tail. He's a good one.'

Now came the hard part of the story, but he had to tell it.

'After Ingrid brought me home, I decided to go back to Spigonella and have a look at the villa.'

'Alone, naturally,' Mimì said sardonically, stirring in his chair.

'I went there alone and I came back alone.'

This time it was Fazio's turn to squirm in his chair. But he didn't open his mouth.

'When Inspector Augello asked you to leave the room,' said Montalbano, turning to him, 'it was because he didn't want you to hear him calling me an arsehole. Would you like to call me one, too? You could form a little chorus.'

'I would never dare, sir.'

'Well, if you don't want to say it, I give you permission to think it.'

Reassured by Fazio's silence and complicity, he described the little harbour, the grotto and the iron door with the internal staircase. He also talked about the crabs that had eaten the flesh off Errera's corpse.

'OK, that's the part that's already happened,' he concluded. 'Now we need to think about a course of action. If the information I've received from Marzilla is correct, tonight there will be more arrivals, and since Zarzis has taken the trouble to come this far, it means there's new merchandise for him on the way. We have to be there the moment it arrives.'

'All right,' said Mimì. 'But, whereas you know everything about this villa, we know nothing about either the villa or its surroundings.'

'Have a look at the video I made of it from the sea. Torrisi's got it.'

'That's not enough. I'm going to go there in person, I want to see for myself,' Mimì decided.

'I don't like it,' Fazio cut in.

'If they spot you and get suspicious, we blow the whole thing,' the inspector seconded him.

'Calm down, both of you. I'll go with Beba, who's been wanting a breath of sea air. We'll take a nice long stroll and see what there is to see. I don't think they'll get alarmed if they see a man and a pregnant woman walking along the beach. We can meet back here by five at the latest.'

'All right,' said Montalbano. Then, turning to Fazio, 'Listen, I want the core squad ready. A few trusted, decisive men. Gallo, Galluzzo, Imbrò, Germanà, and Grasso. You and Augello will be in command.'

'Why, won't you be there?' asked Augello in amazement.

'I'll be there, but I'll be down below, in the little harbour, to stop anyone who tries to escape.'

'Well, Augello will command the squad, 'cause I'm coming with you,' Fazio said dryly.

Surprised by his tone, Mimì glared at him.

'No,' said Montalbano.

'Look, Chief – I—'

'No. This is a personal matter, Fazio.'

This time Mimì glared at Montalbano, who was glaring at Fazio, who was glaring right back. It looked like a scene from a Quentin Tarantino movie, except that they were aiming their eyes instead of guns at each other.

'Yes, sir,' Fazio said at last.

To dispel the bit of tension still in the air, Mimì Augello asked a question:

'How will we know for sure whether or not there will be any landings tonight? Who's going to tell us?'

'You could find out from Commissioner Riguccio,' Fazio suggested to Montalbano. 'They usually have a pretty clear picture of the situation by six pm.'

'No, I've already asked Riguccio too many things. He's a true policeman and might get suspicious. No, I think I know of another way. The harbour authority. They're the ones who receive all the information from the fishermen and patrol boats and pass it on to the commissioner's office. What information there is to be had, that is, since often nobody knows anything about these illegal landings. Do you know anyone at the harbour office?'

'No, Chief.'

'I do,' said Mimì. 'Until last year I used to spend time with a lieutenant from the office, who's still around.'

'Good. When can you go and talk to this guy?'

'This woman, you mean,' Mimì corrected him. 'But

don't get the wrong idea. I tried, but there was nothing doing. We've remained friends. As soon as I get back from Spigonella, I'll take Beba home and go and look her up.'

'And what are we going to do about Marzilla, Chief?'

'After Spigonella, we'll cook his goose along with Aguglia's.'

✻

Opening the refrigerator, he got a nasty surprise. Adelina had tidied up the house as requested, but all she'd made to eat was half a boiled chicken. What kind of bullshit was this? That was a dish for the sick! For someone awaiting last rites! A horrible suspicion occurred to him – that is, that Fazio had told the housekeeper he'd been unwell and therefore should eat lightly. But how could he have told her, if the phone was unplugged? Via carrier pigeon? No, this was clearly some sort of vendetta on Adelina's part, for the mess he'd left the house in. On the kitchen table he found a note he hadn't noticed when he'd made himself coffee.

Youl half to make your bed yourself coz your sleping in it now.

He sat out on the veranda and swallowed down the boiled chicken with the help of an entire jar of pickles. As soon as he'd finished, the phone rang. Apparently Adelina had plugged it back in. It was Livia.

'Salvo, finally! I was so worried! I must have called ten times last night, right up to midnight. Where were you?'

'Sorry. We had to do a stakeout and—'

'I've got some good news for you.'

'Oh? What?'

'I'm coming tomorrow.'

'Really?'

'Yes. I've done and said so much that they gave me three days.'

Montalbano felt a wave of happiness sweep over him.

'So, aren't you going to say something?' asked Livia.

'What time do you get in?'

'Noon. At Punta Raisi.'

'I'll either come myself or send someone to get you. I'm so . . .'

'Come on. Is it so hard for you to say it?'

'No. I'm so happy.'

Before lying down – because he suddenly felt like a nap – he had to tidy up the bedroom or he wouldn't be able to close his eyes.

✣

Mimì straggled back in well past six o'clock, and Fazio came in behind him.

'You took your time, I'd say,' Montalbano chided him.

'But I've got some good stuff.'

'Like what?'

'First of all, these.'

He took ten or so Polaroid snapshots out of his pocket. Every one of them showed a smiling, pregnant

Beba in the foreground, and the villa at Spigonella, shot from every possible angle, in the background. In two or three of them, Beba was actually leaning against the bars of the entrance gate, which was locked shut with a chain and big padlock.

'But did you tell Beba what you were doing there, and who was inside that villa?'

'No. What need was there? This way she acted more naturally.'

'So you didn't see anyone?'

'Maybe they were watching us from inside, but we certainly didn't see anyone outside. They want to give the impression that the house is uninhabited. See that padlock? It's all for show, because one could easily slip a hand through the bars and open the gate from the inside.'

He selected another photo and handed it to the inspector.

'This is the right-hand side of the house. There's an external staircase leading to the upper floor, and that large door below must be the garage. Did Ingrid mention whether the garage is connected to the rest of the house?'

'No, the garage is a separate space without any doors except its entrance. There is, however, an internal staircase between the ground floor and the upstairs, though Ingrid never actually saw it, since the only access to it was through a door D'Iunio said he didn't have the key to. And I'm sure there's another staircase leading from the ground floor down to the grotto.'

'At a glance, the garage looks like it could hold two cars.'

'Well, there's definitely one in there. The one that ran over the little boy. Speaking of which, when we catch these people, I want that car examined by Forensics. I'd bet my family jewels that they find the kid's blood on it.'

'What do you think happened?' Fazio asked.

'Simple. The kid realized – I'm not sure how – that he was up against something horrible. So he tried to escape the minute he got off the boat. It was my fault he didn't succeed on the first try. They took him to Spigonella, and there he must have discovered the staircase leading to the grotto. I'm sure that's how he escaped. Somebody caught on and sounded the alarm. So Zarzis got in the car and looked for him until he found him.'

'But this Zarzis only arrived yesterday!' said Augello.

'As I understand it, Zarzis comes and goes. He's always around when it's time to sort out the merchandise and pick up the money. Like now. He runs all these operations for his boss.'

'I want to talk about the landings,' said Mimì.

'You have the floor,' said Montalbano.

The idea that he had Zarzis within reach gave him a sense of well-being.

'My lady friend told me it's a real state of emergency. Our sea patrols have intercepted four overloaded, dilapidated craft headed towards Seccagrande, Capobianco, Manfia and Fela, respectively. They only hope those boats manage to land before they sink; at this point, re-routing them or transferring the refugees to other vessels is out of the question. All our people can do is stay close behind them and be prepared to rescue the refugees if one or more of the boats should capsize.'

'I get it,' said a pensive Montalbano.

'You get what?' asked Mimì.

'These four landings have been set up as decoys. Seccagrande and Capobianco are to the west of the Vigàta–Spigonella area, and Manfia and Fela are to the east. The sea off Vigàta–Spigonella is therefore momentarily without surveillance, the coast too. Any fishing boat aware of this momentary corridor could easily land on one of our beaches without anyone noticing.'

'So?'

'So, my dear Mimì, that means Zarzis is going to go pick up his merchandise out on the water, with the dinghy. I don't remember if I mentioned that there's a two-way radio inside the villa. With that, they can stay in continuous contact and meet at a fixed spot. Did your lieutenant—'

'She's not mine.'

'Did she tell you what time they were expecting these boats to reach land?'

'Around midnight.'

'That means you and the rest of the team should be ready at Spigonella by ten at the latest. Here's what we'll do. There are two signal lights on the rocks at the entrance to the little harbour. These will come on right before the dinghy goes out, and will be turned on again when it returns. I think these lights, and the moving barrier, are operated by a third man, the guardian of the villa. You're going to have to go easy at first — that is, you can't neutralize the guardian until after, I repeat, after he's turned on the beacons for the dinghy's re-entry. Then you'll have very little time. Once Zarzis and his helper are back in the house, you'll take them by surprise. But be careful: they'll have children with them, and they're capable of anything. Now coordinate your actions between yourselves. I'm going out. Good luck, and may you bear only sons.'

'Where are you going?' asked Augello.

'I'm going back home for a minute, then I'll head out to Spigonella. But let me repeat: you'll be working on your own, and so will I.'

He left the room. Passing Catarella, he asked:

'Cat, could you find out if Torretta has some wire cutters and a pair of thigh-high rubber boots?'

He did. Wire cutters and boots.

*

At home he put on a black turtleneck sweater, a pair of black corduroy trousers, which he tucked into the boots, and a woollen cap, also black, replete with pompom, which he put on his head. All he needed was a bent pipe in his mouth, and he would be a perfect replica of the generic sea dog one often sees in third-rate American movies. He went

to the mirror to have a look at himself. All he could do
was laugh.

'Avast, old salt!'

He got to the white-and-red house in Spigonella by
ten, but instead of turning onto the road to the bungalow,
he took the one he'd taken the first time with Fazio. For
the final stretch, he turned the headlights off. The sky was
overcast, and it was so dark he couldn't see a blasted thing
more than a step away. He got out of the car and looked
around. To the right, a hundred or more yards away, the
villa's dark mass. Of his men, no sign at all. Nothing.
Either they hadn't arrived yet, or if they had, they'd blended
in perfectly. Wire cutters in hand and pistol in his pocket,
he walked along the edge of the cliff until he could make
out the start of the staircase he'd spotted the first time
he was there. It wasn't as hard going down as the other
staircase, either because this one was less steep, or because
he felt reassured to know that his men were nearby.

Halfway down the steps, he heard a motor rumbling.
He realized at once that it was the dinghy, about to head
out to sea. The sound was amplified by the silence and the
grotto, which acted as an echo chamber. He froze. The
water in front of the little harbour suddenly turned red.
From where he stood, Montalbano didn't actually see the
signal light come on, since it was blocked by the tall rock
in front of it. But that red reflection couldn't mean anything
else. He distinctly saw the dinghy's silhouette pass through

the reflection, though he couldn't tell how many people were on board. Then the red glow vanished and the sound of the motor faded, turning into a flylike buzz that went on a long time before it disappeared. Everything was exactly as he'd imagined it. Resuming his descent, he had to refrain from singing at the top of his lungs. So far, he'd made all the right moves.

His satisfaction, however, did not last long. Walking on the dry sand in those high boots immediately proved arduous. Ten more steps, in fact, would have broken his back; on the other hand, moving closer to the water's edge, where the sand was wet and more compacted, would have been too dangerous, taking him too far out in the open. He sat down on the ground and tried to remove the first boot. It slid a little down his thigh, then stubbornly refused to budge past his knee. He stood up and tried again from an upright position. Worse yet. He started sweating and cursing. He finally wedged a heel between two rocks protruding from the wall and managed to free himself. He resumed walking, barefoot, holding the wire cutters in one hand and the enormous boots in the other. In the dark he failed to see a clump of weeds full of thorns and stepped right on top of it. At least a hundred thorns plunged gleefully into the sole of his foot. He felt discouraged. He had to face the facts: these kinds of operations were no longer for him. When he got to the edge of the moat, he sat down on the ground and put the boots back on, breaking into a cold sweat from the pain caused by the friction of the rubber against all the thorns.

Lowering himself gently into the moat, he was pleased to find that he'd guessed right: the water came up to mid-thigh, barely half an inch below the top of the boots. Before him now stood the first of the midget monoliths that formed the little harbour, rising almost directly out of the rock face. Sticking the wire cutters in his belt, he groped the rock's surface and found two protrusions to grab on to. He hoisted himself up with the strength of his arms. The rubber soles of the boots facilitated the climb with their traction. He slipped only once, managing to hang on with a single hand. Scaling the rock like a crab, he reached the wire fence, grabbed the wire cutters and, starting on the lower right, cut the first wire. A crisp, metallic *crack* rang out in the silence like a pistol shot, or so it seemed to him, at least. He held utterly still, not daring to move even a finger. But nothing happened. Nobody shouted, no one came running. Then, *crack* after *crack* – pausing cautiously between *cracks* – after half an hour he had managed to sever all the wires that were welded to the iron pole, which in turn was cemented into the rock face. He left only the top two wires uncut – one on the right, the other on the left – keeping the screen suspended and making it look like it was still intact. He would cut them in due time. For now, he had to get out of there. He left the wire cutters under the screen and, clinging to the upper part of the rock with both hands, he extended his body, searching for a foothold with his feet. Thinking he'd found one, he wedged the toes of his boots in the opening and let go. It was a mistake. The opening was not very deep and could not bear his weight. He slid down the rock, trying to halt the slide by using his fingers as claws. He felt like Sylvester the cat in one of his finest moments. He skinned his hands and plunged straight into the moat. But why didn't Aristotle's, er, Archimedes' principle kick in? This principle said that a body immersed in liquid is buoyed up by a force equal to the weight of liquid displaced. Wasn't that it? Whereas he had in no way been buoyed up. The only thing buoyed up was the water that came flying up over his head and fell back down on him, drenching his sweater and cheerfully flowing down between his balls and into his boots. On top of this, his fall had sounded exactly like a beaching whale to him. He pricked his ears. Again, nothing. No voices, no sounds. Since the sea was a little rough, perhaps the watchman had thought it was merely a bigger wave splashing against the rocks. He climbed up out of the moat and lay down on the sand.

What now? Count from one to a billion? Try to recite from memory every poem he knew? Think of all the possible ways to cook mullet? Start imagining all the reasons he would give to the commissioner and the public prosecutor for having worked on this case on the sly, without 'the authorization of his superiors'? All of a sudden he felt a sneeze coming on, tried to suppress it, did not succeed, but blocked the burst by plugging his nose with his hand.

He felt like he had a pint of water in each boot. All he needed now was a damn cold! On top of everything, he was beginning to feel chilled. He got up and started walking very close to the wall. Too bad if he had a backache tomorrow. After a hundred or so paces, he turned around. When he was back at the moat, he turned round again and retraced his steps. He went back and forth some ten times. Cold? Now he was hot and sweaty. He decided to take a brief rest and sat down on the ground. Then he lay down completely. Half an hour later, a troubling somnolence began to take hold of him. He closed his eyes, then reopened them after a brief spell, he couldn't tell how long, bothered by the buzzing of a large fly.

Fly? That was the dinghy returning! He quickly rolled towards the moat, slid into it standing up but hunched over. The buzzing became a rumble, and the rumble became a roar as the dinghy drew near. Then the roar stopped all at once. The dinghy was certainly now coasting on its momentum as it made its way through the canal and entered the grotto. Montalbano climbed up the rock without any difficulty, drawing strength and lucidity from the assurance that he would soon have the satisfaction he so desired. Once his head was at the level of the wire fence, he saw a great beam of light projecting out of the entrance of the grotto. He also heard two men shouting angrily, and some children crying and whimpering, which wrenched his heart and turned his stomach. Hands sweaty and trembling, not from tension but from rage, he waited for the grotto to fall silent again. When he was about to cut the first of the fence's two remaining wires, the light also went out. A good sign. It meant that the grotto was now empty. He cut the wires without precaution, one after the other, then let the large square of mesh that remained in his hand slide down the rock before dropping it into the moat.

He made his way past the two metal poles, then jumped down onto the sand, in the dark, from the top of the rock. A jump of over ten feet, and the Good Lord let him pull it off. In those last few minutes he felt a good ten years younger. He pulled out his pistol, cocked it and went into the grotto. Total darkness and silence. He walked along the narrow quay until his hand felt the iron door, which was half open. He went inside the hangar and quickly – as if he could see – reached the archway, passed under it, stepped onto the first stair and stopped there. How come everything was so quiet? Why hadn't his men started doing what they were supposed to do? A thought crossed his mind, and he began to sweat: what if they'd hit a snag and hadn't arrived yet? And there he was, in the dark, gun in hand, looking like some dickhead dressed up as a sea dog! Why didn't they get moving? Jesus Christ! Was this some kind of joke? Were Mr Zarzis and his pals going to slip away, just like that? By God, no, even if he had to go up to the villa and raise the roof all by himself.

At that very moment he heard, almost all at once, though muffled in the distance, a burst of pistol shots, machine-gun fire and angry shouts whose words remained incomprehensible. What to do? Wait there or run up to the house and provide support for his men? The shoot-out continued overhead, fierce and sounding as if it was coming closer. Suddenly a very bright light came on at once in the stairway, hangar and grotto. Someone was getting ready to escape. He distinctly heard some hurried steps coming down the staircase. In a flash the inspector ran back through the arch and ducked behind it, back to the wall. A second later, a man came huffing past, popping out with a kind of hop, exactly the way a rat comes out of a sewer.

'Stop! Police!' Montalbano yelled, stepping forward.

The man did not stop but merely turned slightly around, raising his left hand, which held a large pistol, and shot behind himself almost blindly. The inspector felt a fierce blow strike his left shoulder with such force that it turned his whole upper body around to the left. His feet and legs, however, remained in place, rooted to the ground. When the man had reached the door to the garage, Montalbano's first and only shot struck him square between the shoulder blades. The man stopped, threw out his arms, dropped the pistol, and fell face-forward to the ground. The inspector approached slowly, unable to walk any faster, and with the tip of his boot turned the body over.

Jamil Zarzis seemed to smile at him with his toothless mouth.

Somebody had once asked him if he'd ever felt happy

about killing another man. He'd said no. He didn't feel happy this time, either. Gratified, yes. That was exactly the word: gratified.

He knelt down slowly. His legs felt weak, and he had an overwhelming desire to sleep. Blood was pouring out of the wound in his shoulder and soaking his sweater. The shot must have made a big hole.

'Inspector! Oh my God, Inspector! I'll call an ambulance!'

Montalbano's eyes remained closed, but he recognized Fazio's voice.

'No ambulances. Why did you guys take so long to get started?'

'We were waiting while they put the kids in a room, thinking we could move more easily that way.'

'How many of them are there?'

'Seven. It looked like a nursery. They're all OK. We killed one of the men, and another surrendered. You shot the third. That pretty much covers it. Now can I call someone to give me a hand?'

*

When the inspector regained consciousness, he was inside a car with Gallo at the wheel. Fazio was behind him with his arms around him, as the car bounced high along a road full of holes. They had removed his sweater and improvised a temporary bandage over the wound. He felt no pain from it; perhaps that would come later. He tried to speak, but on first try nothing came out, because his lips were too dry.

'... Livia ...'s flying in ... this morning ... Punta Raisi.'

'Don't you worry,' said Fazio. 'One of us will go pick her up, you can count on it.'

'Where are you ... taking me?'

'To Montechiaro hospital. It's the closest.'

Then something happened that Fazio found frightening. He realized that the noise coming from Montalbano was not a cough or him clearing his throat. The inspector was laughing. What was there to laugh about in this situation?

'What's so funny, Chief?' he asked, concerned.

'I wanted to screw ... my guardian angel ... by not going to the doctor ... But he ... screwed me ... by sending me to the hospital.'

Hearing this answer, Fazio got really scared. The inspector was apparently delirious. More terrifying still was the injured Montalbano's sudden yell.

'Stop the car!'

Gallo slammed on the brakes; the car skidded.

'Up there ... is that ... the fork in the road?'

'Yes, Chief.'

'Take the road to Tricase.'

'But, Chief ...' Fazio cut in.

'I said take the road to Tricase.'

Gallo started out slowly, turned right, and then almost at once Montalbano ordered him to stop.

'Put on your brights.'

Gallo obeyed, and the inspector leaned out the car window. The mound of gravel was no longer there. It had been used to level the road.

'It's better this way.'

Suddenly, the wound began to hurt him terribly.

'Let's go to the hospital,' he said.

They drove off.

'Oh, Fazio, another thing...,' he continued with great effort, running a dry tongue over his parched lips, 'don't forget ... don't forget ... to tell Pontius Pilate ... he's at the Hotel Regina.'

Madunnuzza santa! Now he's raving about Pontius Pilate! Fazio humoured him, as one does with the insane.

'Of course we'll tell him, Chief, of course. Just stay calm. I'll do it myself, first thing.'

It was too much of an effort to talk, to explain. Montalbano let himself go, falling into a half swoon. Fazio, all sweaty from the fright these meaningless words were giving him, leaned forward and whispered to Gallo:

'Come on, for Chrissakes, step on it! Can't you see the Chief's not right in the head?'

Author's Note

The names, characters, and situations represented in this novel are, of course, wholly invented.

The statistics on the illegal immigration of minors into Italy, on the other hand, are drawn from an investigation by Carmelo Abbate and Paolo Ciccioli, published in the 19 September 2002 edition of *Panorama*, and the information on the human traffickers derives from an article published in the 26 September 2002 edition of the Italian daily *La Repubblica*. The story of the phoney death was likewise suggested to me by a news item (*Gazzetta del Sud*, 17, 20 and 24 August 2002).

Notes

page 3 – **octopus *a strascinasali* or sardines *a beccafico*** – Octopus *a strascinasali* consists of small octopuses (*polipetti* in Italian, *purpiteddri* or *frajeddi* in Sicilian) simply boiled in salted water, then dressed in olive oil and lemon juice. *Sarde a beccafico* is a famous Sicilian speciality named after a small bird, the *beccafico* (*Sylvia borin*, garden warbler in English), which is particularly fond of figs (*beccafico* means 'fig-pecker'). The headless, cleaned sardines are stuffed with sautéed breadcrumbs, pine nuts, sultanas and anchovies, then rolled up in such a way that they resemble the bird when they come out of the oven.

page 4 – **the police raid of the Diaz School during the G8 meetings in Genoa** – The G8 meetings held in Genoa, Italy, in July 2001, were marred by unusual violence by the forces of order against protesters, culminating in the shooting dead of a young man who had threatened a group of carabinieri with a fire extinguisher. Among the brutal police tactics was the night-time raid of the Diaz School, where a number of protesters and independent journalists were staying. All of the details related by Camilleri in regard to this event, including his assertion that high functionaries of the police bureaucracy were involved in the Diaz raid, are true and well documented in the mainstream press. Many of those attacked by police during the raid, including British freelance journalist Mark Covell, were severely injured; others were taken from the school to a temporary detention centre called Bolzaneto, where they were subjected to further beatings and humiliation. Two separate trials against no fewer than seventy-three members of police, carabinieri, and prison officers were ongoing as of December 2005, with charges including abuse of authority and unlawful violence, as well as trespass, false arrest, inflicting or authorizing grievous bodily harm, not to mention fabricating the evidence intended to justify the raid at the Diaz School.

page 4 – **as the government watchfully looked on** – Prime Minister Silvio Berlusconi, a media tycoon in his own right, was known to exercise tight control on the news and information propagated in private as well as state-owned media.

page 4 – **brought to mind long-buried episodes of the Fascist police or the Scelba period** – Minister of the interior during successive post-war governments from 1947 to 1953, Mario Scelba (1901–1991) was a fierce anti-communist known for his brutal repression of demonstrations and his use of the police and anti-riot squads to that end.

page 9 – **Imagine ever finding any obscene graffiti in Sicily without the word 'cuckold' in it!** – The Italian word for cuckold, *cornuto*, a common insult throughout the country, is a special favourite among southerners, Sicilians in particular.

page 11 – **solitary walks along the jetty … hours spent sitting on the rock of tears** – As described in earlier books in this series, the inspector is fond of taking solitary walks along the jetty in the port of Vigàta. Under the lighthouse at the end of the jetty, there is a rock, one of the many that make up the breakwater, on which he likes to sit to collect his thoughts. It was on this rock that he first came to terms with his father's death and wept for him, whence the name, the 'rock of tears'. (See A. Camilleri, *The Snack Thief* and subsequent books in the series.)

page 11 – càlia e simenza – A mix of chickpeas and pumpkin seeds, and sometimes peanuts. There is a shop at the start of the jetty that sells this snack, often an integral part of Montalbano's solitary walks. (See previous note.)

page 27 – **'My husband Angelo and I are both from Treviso'** – Treviso is in the Veneto region of north-eastern Italy, one of the strongholds of the Northern League, a right-wing, anti-Southern political party.

page 31 – **L'Avvenire** and **Famiglia Cristiana** – *L'Avvenire* (which means 'The Future') is a Catholic daily; *Famiglia Cristiana* is a weekly magazine published by the Catholic Church.

page 32 – **E passeranno i giorni** – 'And the days will go by.' A line from the aria 'Ch'ella mi creda', in *La Fanciulla del West*, an opera by Giacomo Puccini (1858–1924).

page 33 – **Nothing but angels up there** – Aside from observing that all the persons are named either Angelo or Angela, Montalbano is making a wry comment on the staunch Catholicism for which the people of the Veneto are well known, and on the hypocrisy that allows them to consider themselves more virtuous than the Sicilians.

page 41 – **'Here, Ingrid ... I can't keep up with you'** – Ingrid is a former racing-car driver. (See A. Camilleri, *The Shape of Water*.)

page 55 – **the inspector thought of François, the Tunisian boy who could have become his son...** – See A. Camilleri, *The Snack Thief* and *Voice of the Violin*.

page 62 – **Cozzi–Pini law** – A thinly disguised reference to the Bossi–Fini law, conceived by Umberto Bossi and Gianfranco Fini, respective leaders of the xenophobic Northern League and the National Alliance, a right-wing party descended directly from the neo-Fascist MSI party founded after World War II. Enacted in 2002 by the Italian Parliament, with the ruling coalition of Prime Minister Silvio Berlusconi's Forza Italia party and these two smaller parties holding an absolute majority, this heavy-handed law, among its many provisions: (1) makes it illegal for individuals not belonging to European Union member nations to enter the country without a work contract; (2) requires all non–E.U. individuals who lose their jobs while in the country to repatriate to their country of origin; (3) abolishes the sponsorship system that had previously enabled non–E.U. individuals to enter the country under the patronage of a sponsor already in Italy; (4) establishes the government's right to decree a quota of the number of non–E.U. individuals allowed to enter the country over the period of one year; and (5) makes all foreign nationals not in conformity with these new guidelines subject to criminal proceedings and/or forced repatriation.

page 68 – **De Rege brothers** – Guido ('Bebè') De Rege (1891–1945) and Giorgio ('Ciccio') De Rege (1894–1948) were a celebrated slapstick comedy team of the thirties and forties who performed their routines in variety theatres and in the variety shows that often preceded the screening of films. Perhaps their most famous routine was their oft-repeated opening act, when Bebè, alone on the stage, would look to the wings and say '*Vieni* *avanti, cretino!'* ('Come out here, idiot!'), whereupon his brother would enter, stammering and babbling nervously until he inevitably blurted out some bit of comically ingenious nonsense.

page 70 – *u zù Stefanu* – Uncle Stefano, in Sicilian.

page 71 – **Capo Passero** – Cape at the south-eastern tip of Sicily, near the island of the same name (Isola di Capo Passero).

page 72 – **Pachino** – A town near the south-eastern tip of Sicily, near Capo Passero.

page 94 – **The dust or the altar, that was the question** – A reference to the poem 'Il cinque maggio' ('May the Fifth') by Alessandro Manzoni (1785–1873), dedicated to Napoleon and written upon hearing the news of his death on 5 May 1821. The key passage:

> *tutto ei provò: la gloria*
> *maggior dopo il periglio,*
> *la fuga e la vittoria,*
> *la reggia e il tristo esiglio;*
> *due volte nella polvere,*
> *due volte sull'altar.*

> [he went through it all: greater
> glory after danger, flight
> and victory, the palace royal
> and unhappy exile;
> twice in the dust,
> twice on the altar.]

page 106 – **Road Police** – The Road Police (*Polizia Stradale*) are a separate branch of the Italian police forces.

page 121 – **"*Tutto va ben, mia nobile marchesa*"** – 'All goes well, my noble marchesa.' A sarcastic song from the Fascist period, performed by a well-known musical revue, which alluded ironically to the fact that everything was going quite badly.

page 128 — **It was time to eat. Since most people were at home ...** — In Italy, especially in the South, many people leave work to go home for their lunch break (often three hours long).

page 131 — **Signora Cappuccino in person** — Although this woman is the wife of Gaetano Marzilla, in Sicily she may be called by either her maiden name (Cappuccino) or her married name (Marzilla). This is a remnant of the Spanish custom of a wife's preserving her maiden name as part of her full name after marriage. Sicily, like much of southern Italy, was under Spanish rule for centuries.

page 154 — **a politician killed by the Red Brigades** — A reference to Aldo Moro, kidnapped and murdered by the Red Brigades, an armed revolutionary group, in 1978.

page 158 — **rotating the forefinger of his left hand, gesturing 'later, later'** — This is a common Italian hand gesture. The hand is held horizontally, with the forward rotation of the forefinger implying the passage of time.

page 162 — *Matre santa* — Holy Mother (Sicilian dialect).

page 210 — *Heri dicebamus* — (Lat.) 'Yesterday we were saying.'

page 213 — **Durazzo** — Port city in western Albania.

page 216 — *americanate* — This is the plural of *americanata*, a slang term roughly meaning a grandiose, somewhat unlikely endeavour of the sort that Americans are typically thought to engage in. In reference to film, it might translate as 'American pulp'.

NOTES

page 218 – **the province's remaining insane asylum** – In the 1980s, the majority of Italy's state-run mental hospitals were closed due to lack of funding.

page 232 – **Now shalt thou prove thy mettle** – '*Qui si parrà la tua nobilitate*': Dante, *Inferno* II, line 9, in which the poet exhorts his own memory to rise to the task remembering the marvels he has seen.

page 237 – *ragioniere* **Gargano's** – See A. Camilleri, *The Scent of the Night*.

page 238 – **landsknechts** – seventeenth- and eighteenth-century German mercenary soldiers known for their unruly behaviour.

page 247 – **the air he was breathing had a rotten yellow colour** – As seen in several other books in the series, starting with *The Terracotta Dog*, Inspector Montalbano has the synaesthetic ability to envision smells as colours.

Notes by Stephen Sartarelli